SHADOWS BEYOND THE GATE

SummerHill Secrets

✣ ✣

Whispers Down the Lane
Secret in the Willows
Catch a Falling Star
Night of the Fireflies
A Cry in the Dark
House of Secrets
Echoes in the Wind
Hide Behind the Moon
Windows on the Hill
Shadows Beyond the Gate

SUMMERHILL SECRETS

SHADOWS BEYOND THE GATE

Beverly Lewis

BETHANY HOUSE PUBLISHERS
MINNEAPOLIS, MINNESOTA 55438

Shadows Beyond the Gate
Copyright © 2000
Beverly Lewis

Cover illustration by Chris Ellison
Cover design by the Lookout Design Group, Inc.

Unless otherwise identified, Scripture quotations are from the HOLY BIBLE, NEW INTERNATIONAL VERSION®. Copyright © 1973, 1978, 1984 by International Bible Society. Used by permission of Zondervan Publishing House. All rights reserved. The "NIV" and "New International Version" trademarks are registered in the United States Patent and Trademark Office by International Bible Society. Use of either trademark requires the permission of International Bible Society.

Published by Bethany House Publishers
A Ministry of Bethany Fellowship International
11400 Hampshire Avenue South
Minneapolis, Minnesota 55438
www.bethanyhouse.com

Printed in the United States of America by
Bethany Press International, Minneapolis, Minnesota 55438

Library of Congress Cataloging-in-Publication Data

Lewis, Beverly, 1949–
    Shadows beyond the gate / by Beverly Lewis.
        p. cm. — (Summerhill secrets ; 10)
    Summary: When the wounds from an old tragedy reopen, Merry gradually learns that storms don't last forever and that with God's help she can face the future without her twin sister.
    ISBN 1–55661–876–X (pbk.)
    [1. Grief—Fiction. 2. Twins—Fiction. 3. Christian life—Fiction.] I. Title.
PZ7.L5864 Sh   2000
[Fic]—dc21   99–050589
                                                  CIP

Special thanks
to
Gordon and Betty Bernhardt,
who shared with me
the story of Buttercup,
the *real* twin lamb.

For
Julie Arno,
who heralds herself a
"Sincere SUMMERHILL SECRETS Series Fanatic."

Hide me in the shadow
of your wings . . .

—Psalm 17:8

ONE

Right off the bat, I'll admit that I'd only *thought* I was over the loss of my twin sister. Some days, Faithie's death seems like a long time ago. Other days, it's like yesterday that the leukemia came and took her away.

But the day everything got stirred up again—or got me "all but ferhoodled," as my Amish girl friend would say—was as perfect as any Pennsylvania springtime. It was late May, and the remnants of my freshman year at James Buchanan High were fading all too quickly. Not a single cloud cluttered the clear blue sky.

Rachel Zook came running up SummerHill Lane just as I stepped off the school bus. I took one look at her and knew something was wrong. Her white head covering had tipped a bit off-center, and her usual long gray apron was mussed. Nearly breathless and eyes wide, she sputtered her request, "Can ya come . . . help me out, Merry?"

"You can count on me." I scurried down the road toward the long dirt lane that led to the Zooks' farmhouse, trying to keep up with Rachel, the hem of her skirt flapping in the warm breeze.

"My twin lamb's gonna die, I'm afraid," she said as we ran.

"What's wrong with her?"

"Well, her mama died yesterday morning, just hours after she birthed the twins . . . and then 'twasn't long and the first twin lamb upped and died, too." Rachel stopped running as we neared the barnyard. Catching our breaths, we strolled over to the white plank fence.

I shaded my eyes with my hand as I scanned the grassy, fenced area. "Where is she?"

We searched the corral with our eyes. At last, Rachel located her. "*Ach*, of all things—she's right here."

Peering down through the fence slats, I spied a single baby lamb, all fluffy and white. "Oh, she's so adorable."

"Adorable, *jah*, but she's all alone in the world. Won't eat nothin', neither," Rachel said, her voice

10

soft and low. "We can't get her to take milk, not even from Ol' Nanna."

I was surprised to hear it because I'd seen Ol' Nanna with her own babies. The older sheep was gentle and loving—the way a good foster mother ought to be.

Rachel pointed to Ol' Nanna grazing by herself across the meadow. "She doesn't mind sharin' her milk with young'uns that ain't hers. I can't begin to count the number of orphan lambs we've bonded on to her. And plenty-a time, too." Rachel shook her head. "But not *this* time. It just ain't workin' out."

I stared down at the poor little creature. Her fleece was creamy white, like detergent suds. Made you want to reach down and pick her up—cuddle her like a human baby. My heart went out to the lost lamb. "Why do you think she won't eat?" I asked.

Rachel's fingers trailed down the long white strings of her *Kapp*, the prayer veiling she always wore. She moved close to me, whispering. "If ya want my opinion, I think she's dyin' of loneliness."

I looked out over the enclosure where at least twenty sheep roamed the pastureland, wondering how on earth the lamb could be lonely. "But look at all her relatives. She's got oodles of aunts, uncles, and cousins . . . doesn't she?"

Rachel didn't smile. She frowned instead. "It's the oddest thing, really. But I think she downright misses her twin . . . and her mama." Rachel's voice grew even softer. "If something doesn't change, and soon, I'm afraid she'll just lie down and die. Just plain give up."

Squatting to get closer, I stroked the animal's soft wool coat. Seemed to me, Rachel might be right. "See how her eyes just plead?"

"Like she needs someone to help her, ain't so?" Rachel said. "That's just why I asked ya over here, Merry. I thought you could coax her to take some milk . . . from this baby bottle, maybe." She handed the bottle to me.

"Me?"

"Jah." She paused, and a peculiar look swept across her pretty face. "If ya think on it, I'm sure you'll understand why." She didn't say more but headed off toward the barn, waving that she'd be back "awful quick."

I had to stop and really ponder what Rachel had just said. Kneeling in the grass, I was nearly nose to nose with the adorable animal. "You're such a pretty thing," I said through the fence. I stroked the fleecy coat, cooing at her like I often did to each of my four cats.

Then, while I continued to pet the lamb, I realized exactly what my Amish girl friend meant. It struck me like lightning hits a tree. I *was* a good choice for her lamb project. A very good one, in fact. Because I, too, had suffered great loss. Of course, my twin hadn't died at birth, or even close to it, but Faithie was gone all the same.

I kept watch over the poor, suffering lamb, observing her sad face, the way she could hardly raise her eyes to look at me. She was just too downhearted to think about living, let alone care about drinking milk from a bottle.

"You poor thing," I said softly, offering the baby bottle. When the lamb wasn't interested, I didn't coax. "I think I know what you need."

Setting the bottle down, I turned and sat in the grass. "I think you need a pretty name—one to match who you are."

After a good deal of thinking on my part, an idea came. I whispered the name into the air, imagining the warm breeze picking it up and carrying it high over the silo on the Zooks' bank barn, on past the pond with its bottomless holes, and beyond the creaky windmill.

Yes, it might well be the perfect name. And one way to cheer up a sad little lamb. Sighing, I said, "I think your name should be . . . Jingle Belle. Jingle, for short. What do you think of that?"

At first, I wondered if I might be dreaming, because Jingle suddenly began to respond to her new name. I actually thought she was beginning to smile. Well, sort of, because I guess lambs don't really smile. Unless, of course, they want to.

Jingle shook her head playfully, which rang the little bell at her neck. A sweet, cheerful ringing sound. *Jingle Belle*. What a terrific name. One-hundred-percent-amen wonderful!

It was the sweetest thing—the absolutely nicest thing that had happened to me in a long time. Sitting there in the thick green grass, I leaned against the fence and knew that Rachel would be delighted, too. Yep, things were about to change for her little lamb.

And something else. I couldn't be sure, really, but I had a funny feeling that things were about to change for me, too. Because deep inside, where no one ever sees but God, I still longed for Faithie. It was as if a shadow covered everything on the path of my future.

"Only time will heal that kind of wound," Dad gently reminds me every so often. But I honestly did't see how that could ever be. Half of me is gone. Faithie's absence is like thick pollen in springtime, scattered everywhere.

Leaning my head against the fence, I felt Jingle's soft wool on my forehead. Sweet and comforting, I let her nuzzle me.

Closing my eyes, I allowed my tears to spill out. "I know how you feel, Jingle," I whispered. "And I'm going to help you. I promise."

TWO

On a really warm day, you ought to be able to sit outside in pajamas and play with your cats. Soak up some sunshine. At least, that was my idea of a lazy Saturday morning in SummerHill. But my mother had other plans for me, and I worried that spring would slip through my fingers before I had a chance to do anything truly frivolous.

"We'll sit in the sun another time, little boys," I told Shadrach, Meshach, and Abednego, the cat brothers. I discarded my bathrobe and headed into my walk-in closet to see what to wear.

When I was dressed for the day, I noticed Lily White—the only lady of the feline group—still lying at the foot of my bed. She opened her tiny eyes and blinked, then succumbed again to morning drowsiness. I laughed at her, ignoring her disinterest. "I

know, I know . . . you're not a morning person."
Then, catching myself, I realized what I'd just said.
"Yee-ikes! You're not a *person* at all!"

To that, she opened both eyes wide, stretched
her petite hind legs, and jumped off my bed, pad-
ding slowly toward me.

"Well, what's this?" I said, still laughing at my
adorable white kitten. "Are you up for good?"

She followed me down the hall to my parents'
bedroom, where my mother was busy gathering up
laundry. The washing was probably the reason Mom
had nixed my idea of whiling away the morning in
the sun. Laundry, it seemed, could never wait. It *had*
to be attended to in a timely manner. Which meant
the notion that dirty clothes might merely lie patiently in a hamper until a designated weekly wash
day—like the Amish folk do it—was out of the question. At least at our house. If so much as two days
of washing were to pile up, Mom was on to it like a
cat after a mouse.

"Let's get our work done before noon, what do
you say?" Mom suggested, her hair neatly combed.
She wore her pretty blue blouse and her best casual
pants. I had a feeling she was going out later.

"What's the rush?" I asked.

"Oh, there's an antique show in the area," she

muttered, her arms filling up with Dad's shirts. "That's all."

That's all.

Funny she said it that way, because I knew about Mom's great fascination with antiques. And there was no hiding it. Her interest had become stronger with the passing of each year.

I stumbled after her, my own arms loaded down. "Are you looking for a specific piece?"

"Not for me personally," she said as we made our way downstairs through the kitchen toward the cellar steps.

It seemed to me she didn't really want to say what she was looking for. So I changed the subject. "After I help with the laundry, is it okay if I just hang out for the rest of the afternoon?"

"Hang out?" She pushed Dad's shirts into the washer. "As in *hang out* the clothes to dry?" She wore an affected smile, which quickly faded.

I should've known Mom would think I was volunteering. In her opinion, there was not a more pleasant smell than clothing dried by the fresh air and sunshine.

"Hang out the clothes? Well, no," I said, "that's not what I meant, but . . ."

She eyed me curiously. "You didn't mean to say

that you were going to *waste* away your Saturday afternoon, did you?"

I wondered if my mother would ever understand that what I said most of the time didn't have anything to do with what I *meant* to say. I sighed. "I thought I'd spend some time with Rachel Zook today. That's all."

"Well, why didn't you say so?" Mom replied, turning on the washer and pouring in a cup of detergent.

The suds reminded me of Rachel's little lamb, but I couldn't bring myself to tell Mom about yet another "mammal mission," as she so often referred to my attraction to strays or other pitiful pets.

I thought more about Jingle Belle. Such a sad situation. But it wasn't like I wanted to offer the lamb a roof over her fleecy head. And I didn't want to have her sleep at the bottom of my bed with the cats, and I certainly didn't want to have her following me around inside the house all day. No, I just wanted to help give her the courage to live. Nothing more.

"Okay, Merry," Mom said, jolting me out of my thoughts. "I think it's time we have some breakfast."

If you've never had Saturday breakfast at our house, you have no idea what Mom's idea of "breaking a fast" was all about. To her, it meant cooking up more than enough food for the entire rest of the day!

So while the washing machine did its thing, Mom whipped up waffle batter, fried German sausage and eggs, and made French toast in the oven. I set the table and arranged the homemade jellies and jams (thanks to Esther Zook, Rachel's mother). Then I scurried off to check on my cats . . . and Dad.

I found him reading the paper in his study, still wearing a bathrobe. "I hope you're hungry," I whispered, poking my head around the corner.

He looked up and grinned at me. "Is your mother cooking up a storm?"

"It's Saturday, right?" I laughed, settling into the chair across from his desk. "She'll expect us to sample everything, you know."

Folding his paper, he focused his attention on me. "Your mother has some very interesting plans for herself."

"Yeah, she told me. She's off to an antique show."

He nodded his head. "I didn't mean just her plans for *today*."

"What, then?"

"She's talking of converting our potting shed into an antique shop."

This was news to me. Not once since Dad's early

retirement had I ever stopped to think that we might need additional money each month. But with my older brother, Skip, off at college, maybe we *were* short of cash. "Are we . . . I mean, does Mom need to work?"

His hearty laugh brought some relief for me. "No, no, your mother doesn't need to work. We're fine, honey." He paused, getting up and standing near his chair. "I think your mother's just getting her second wind. That's all."

Not sure what he was talking about, I waited for more.

"She's a bit restless at this stage of her life, I guess you could say. You and your brother are nearly raised, so her interests are beginning to broaden."

"But she's always loved antiques, so this is nothing new."

He fell silent, still holding the folded newspaper in his hands.

"Why would she want an antique shop in our backyard? Doesn't she realize it could be an absolute nightmare—tourists tromping all across our lawn," I spouted. "What's this *really* about?"

Dad came and pulled me up out of the chair gently. "I think your mother's ready to compete with our Amish neighbors."

I was the one chuckling this time. Amish roadside stands couldn't be the reason. "Mom's not going to sell jams and jellies or make quilts, is she?"

"Who knows what she'll sell in her shop." Dad seemed a bit guarded about Mom's ambitions.

"But this is her idea, right?"

He hugged me and guided me down the hall toward the kitchen. "We'll talk more later, okay?"

"Sure," I said, my curiosity piqued. "Later."

❧ ❧

The morning was balmy, with a hint of a shower in the air. Rachel and her sisters, Nancy, Ella Mae, and little Susie, were outside urging the tiny lamb to drink when I arrived at the Zooks' farm.

"How's Jingle doing?" I asked, leaning on the fence post.

"About the same," Nancy said. But the somber look on her face gave her away. The Amish sisters were just as worried as before.

"So . . . nothing's changed?" I pressed.

Rachel shook her head. "Here, *you* try, Merry. Let's see if Jingle will drink for you."

I shrugged, accepting the baby bottle. Hesitant to hunker down and force the poor thing in front of an insistent group, I sat in the grass about two feet from the fence. "Has she ever been let out?" I asked, referring to the fenced area.

Little Susie gasped, cupping her hand over her mouth in horror. "Ach, no, Merry! Jingle might run away and get herself lost. We wouldn't want that to happen, now, would we?"

"No, Susie," Rachel said quickly, comforting her small sister.

Clearly, the youngest Zook was not in favor of my idea. "I didn't mean that Jingle should run loose," I explained to Susie. Then, turning to Rachel, I asked, "What if the lamb came outside the fence—right here with me?" I patted the grass.

Rachel was nodding. Her smile spread across her tan face. "I'd say it's an awful *gut* idea, Cousin Merry." She liked to call me "cousin" because of our distant connection with the same Plain relative.

Usually, I had to smile at her reference to our remote kinship, but not today. Today, something very important was on my mind. Unlike my mother's idea to run an antique shop out of a backyard shed, *I* hoped to get a lonely and dying lamb's full attention. Because maybe today Jingle Belle would nurse from the bottle for me. I could only hope . . . and pray.

THREE

Before she embarked on her antique adventure, Mom stopped by the Zooks' house. There was a familiar glint in her eye as she leaned her head out the car window. "Merry, honey, I thought you'd like to know. Jonathan Klein called just as I was leaving the house."

Jon! My heart jittered.

"What did he want?" I asked.

She touched one delicate blue earring, a grin adding even more pizzazz to her outfit. "He wanted to talk to *you*. But since I told him you were over here, he said he'll call you later, in about an hour."

I glanced at my watch. "Good . . . that's perfect." I would be sure to make it home by then.

Mom looked tired. No, she looked totally wiped out. I watched her drive the car forward, creeping into the barnyard area. As she came back around, I flagged her down, stopping her. "You okay?" I asked, leaning on the car window.

"Just a little tired," she said, shrugging. "I'll take a nap later."

A nap? Mom *never* took naps!

"Will you please take it easy?" I asked.

She nodded. "Don't miss your phone call," she said, blowing a kiss. She headed down the long dirt road and was still waving out the car window as she made the turn onto SummerHill Lane.

I giggled at her girlish approach to *my* love life. Yep, Mom was on to something. Tired or not. Most likely she'd guessed how much I liked the former Wordplay Wizard from James Buchanan High. Jon Klein and I had discarded our alliteration absurdity. Yet I still found myself creating phrases with matching vowels or consonants, almost at will. The difference was that I wasn't constantly *trying* to alliterate when Jon and I were together. And neither was Jon. Our friendship was secure and strong, much better now that we weren't hung up on trying to impress each other with our wits.

Turning back to the task at hand, I was glad Rachel and her sisters had slipped away into the house. I suspected they were helping their mother with baking bread and pies for church. Tomorrow was their turn to have Preaching service at their house.

Meanwhile, I had loosely tied the little lamb to one of the fence posts. It was the post nearest a young willow tree. An eight-year-old tree, to be exact. I knew its age to the day because I'd sat in the grass the afternoon it had been planted—though by accident.

I'd never heard of a fishing pole becoming a tree. Stories like that came from tall tales. Some of the Old Order Plain folk were known for such entertaining yarns, but the truth was this: Faithie's willow stick—her fishing pole—actually grew a tree. I never forgot the surprise on her ashen face, weeks later, when that skinny pole began to sprout in our Amish neighbors' yard!

The long-ago August day had been so exciting for Faithie and me—two little "English" girls spending the day on an Amish dairy farm. We'd gone fishing with the older Zook kids, hoping to bring home at least one small fish for our mother to cook in the frying pan. After all, Levi Zook and his big brother, Curly John, caught fish like that all the time.

On that particular day, Levi and Rachel—both a few years older than my sister and me—helped us hook our bait. They showed us the best place to cast our lines. But it was my twin sister's determination to catch a fish that spurred me on. By afternoon's end, neither one of us had caught anything, but that didn't dampen Faithie's spirits. She wanted to come back and try the next day. Except that it was the Lord's Day, so we knew better than to ask Daddy's permission.

"We'll go fishin' again next week," Levi had said, wearing Curly John's baggy hand-me-downs.

"I think my willow stick's too green," Faithie had told us, laughing as we tromped toward the barn, away from the pond.

"Maybe that's why the fish wouldn't bite today," I said, not knowing for sure. After all, we were young—just one month shy of six years old.

"Better get yourself a sturdier stick next time," Rachel offered, pointing to a hint of green beneath the bark.

"Jah, gut thinkin'," Levi said, waving as he headed for the house.

Rachel stood and talked with us a bit longer, lingering near the fenced area. There weren't any new lambs that year—at least I don't remember them. If there had been, I'm sure Faithie and I would've leaned on the fence, coaxing one of the soft little ones over so we could pet it. Faithie and I were both crazy about animals.

When Rachel's mother called for supper, Rachel

hurried off to the house. I figured we'd be heading home soon. But for some reason, Faithie wanted to sit in the grass and "watch the sheep."

"What for?" I'd asked, sitting next to her.

"Just 'cause."

So we sat there, gawking at the Zooks' sheep. Faithie told me a strange story that afternoon. Not a tall tale or anything like that. But she shared something of her young heart with me while she fooled with her fishing pole, pushing it down . . . down ever so slowly into the ground.

"Know what, Merry?" she began.

"What?"

"Last night I dreamed we had our tenth birthday."

I giggled at that. "That's silly."

"But ten's a long time away, isn't it?" Faithie said, still pushing on her fishing pole.

Turning ten *had* seemed like a lifetime away! Besides that, girls who were ten were nearly grown-up. At least, it seemed that way. We didn't talk about that so much, though. It was the birthday thing, the passing of years, that was most heavy on Faithie's mind.

"Birthdays are weird," she continued.

"Huh?"

"You change to a new number." She sighed, letting go of the fishing pole. "But when you're seven, you're still six inside. And five and four and three— all the *old* birthdays wrapped up in the next number. Uncle Tim was in my dream, too. He explained all this to me."

I didn't really get what she was saying. Besides, it seemed weird to me, especially because our uncle was dead. "What do you think Uncle Tim meant?"

"He *told* me when you're six or seven or eight, you're still five and four and three inside." She looked frustrated, as if she was struggling to explain.

I thought about what she'd said. "Do you mean sometimes you wanna cuddle your teddy bear . . . so it's like you're still two years old or even only one?"

Faithie started giggling. "That's it! When you act like a three-year-old, you still *are* that number. And when you set the table for Mommy and do something more grown-up, you're four or five, too. All at the same time."

"How old will we feel when we're ten, I wonder?"

Suddenly, her eyes were big and round. "Maybe we won't feel different at all."

"We'll have to just wait and see," I said.

She looked pleased with herself. Like she'd finally made her dream clear to me. "Having birthdays is like tiny puzzle pieces all fit together. Uncle

Tim said one year goes inside the next."

"Wow. Uncle Tim's very smart since he's gone to heaven."

"I think so, too." Then she kissed me all over my face, knocking me down in the tall green grass.

"What age are you now?" I teased.

By the time we left for home, the fishing pole was stuck in the hole. "Leave it there," Faithie had said, patting the ground around it. "Maybe it'll sprout someday."

I laughed, wondering where on earth my sister had gotten such an idea.

❧ ❧

A clap of thunder startled me, and I rushed to get the lamb back inside the fence. Jingle had taken only a small amount of milk from the bottle. That didn't mean she wouldn't eventually get used to the bottle. Because I was *not* giving up!

After getting the lamb back inside the fold, I ran to take shelter. On the Zooks' front porch, I watched the rain come pelting down, spawned by a determined cloudburst. The lone willow swayed, keeping company with the wind.

Maybe we won't feel different at all. . . .

How sad that Faithie hadn't lived to experience her tenth birthday; not even her eighth. And yet the seven years we had together were mighty strong in me. I would never forget them. Or her.

More than that, I felt incomplete without my sister. Like a tree that has shed its leaves in the autumn, I still felt bare without her. Something would always be missing for me. I'd read that all twins feel that way if separated at birth or if one of them dies. Well, it was definitely one-hundred-percent-amen true!

Staring out over the grassy meadow, I spotted the frail little lamb. Her ribs poked through her sides. It pained me to see how scrawny she was. Sighing, I understood how she must feel, losing both her mother and twin sister. She needed a reason to live, to want to take nourishment.

It was then, as I stood on the Zooks' long white front porch, in the midst of a midday thunder-shower, I knew exactly what I must do. As soon as possible!

FOUR

I borrowed Rachel's umbrella for the walk home. The rain was still coming down fast, but I couldn't let it stop me. I was anxious to get home for Jon's phone call, so I hurried down the Zooks' lane as the dirt quickly turned into a muddy path.

While I was removing my muddy shoes at our back door, I heard the phone ring. Dad would answer. No rush.

"I'm home if it's for me!" I called, coming inside.

Sure enough, the ringing stopped in the middle of the second ring. I waited, holding my breath . . . hoping. Was it Jon calling?

When I didn't hear my name, I assumed the call was for Dad and headed upstairs to my room. I removed my soggy socks and greeted my cats. All four of them were huddled inside my closet. I didn't blame them for hiding, not after those amazingly powerful claps of thunder. And poor Abednego . . . well, I'm sure it brought back harrowing memories of the day he ran away from home. All because of a vicious storm.

"You okay, kitties?" I cooed, getting down on my hands and knees to nuzzle each of them. "Thunder never hurt anybody."

Abednego was trembling so hard, I picked him up, fat and heavy as he was. "Aw, little man, it'll be all right. Merry's here with you."

Lily White wasn't impressed with the attention my eldest cat was receiving. She pushed her face against my hand, and I decided it was time to dish out equal time. So I sat on the floor of my closet, with the only light filtering in from the bedroom, talking baby talk to my cats. "Let's pretend we're only three years old," I caught myself saying. "So it's okay if we're scared, right?"

Of course, I wasn't really that frightened by the thunder or the storm. But it comforted the cats to see me calm and in control.

While I petted Lily White, I glanced up at the shelf above me. Scrapbooks of Faithie and me stood neatly in a row. Did I dare open them today? Stir up even more memories? I wondered if possibly my memories of Faithie's illness might help me nurse

Jingle Belle back to health. Maybe I *should* take a peek, I decided. It had been quite a while since I'd cozied up with one of the scrapbooks.

Just as I was putting Lily White down, I heard Dad calling up the stairs. "Merry! Kiddo, the phone's for you."

I could hardly believe my ears. Had Dad been talking to Jon Klein all this time?

"Coming," I said, leaving my cat foursome to deal with the storm on their own. I hurried to Skip's bedroom, just down the hallway from my room. Not wanting to sound too eager, I counted to five before I picked up the phone.

Jon was happy to hear my voice. At least, he *sounded* upbeat and happy. "Hi, Merry. What're you doing today?"

"Hanging with my cats right now. Before that, I was over at Rachel Zook's."

"That's cool."

I had to know, so I asked. "Were you talking to my dad, uh, before?"

"Yeah, he was giving me some pointers on my new camera. Nice guy, your dad." Then Jon began to tell me about his latest photography project. "This class I'm taking is really great. Mostly outdoor shots . . . nature, trees . . . stuff like that."

"Sounds fun," I replied, thinking that he should

come out to SummerHill and take pictures of the new lamb. But no, I didn't want to invite him. Not yet.

"Would you like to go with me—with the youth group—next Tuesday night?" he asked.

"Where to?"

"Hiking . . . ending up at the youth pastor's house for ice cream sundaes."

I wasn't sure what shape Rachel's lamb might be in by next week. "I'll have to see," I said, holding back.

He was silent for a second, then—"Everything okay?"

"It's just that I might be busy, that's all."

"Too busy for a hike?" There were more questions in his voice, but he didn't push.

"I'll have to let you know," I said. "Thanks for calling."

After we hung up, I worried that he might've thought I didn't want to go. But I wasn't concerned enough to call back.

And at church the next day, I didn't say a word about the lamb, either. I guess I felt it was just my thing . . . this sickly lamb and me. My thing and God's.

❧   ❧

The next time Jon called was Monday evening. I'd totally forgotten to get back to him about the hike. But I wasn't home when he called, so Mom took another message.

"Are things all right between you and your friend?" Mom asked, her eyes searching mine. "Seems like you're playing phone tag."

I went to the sink to wash my hands. "I've got other things on my mind," I said.

"Not Levi Zook, I hope," Mom shot back.

Why she had that idea, I didn't know. "Levi's off at college," I reminded her.

"I heard he's coming home for a visit." Mom pulled a chair away from the table and sat down. No doubt she wanted to talk this through.

"Are you sure? Because last I heard, he wasn't."

She frowned. "Miss Spindler told me just today that he was."

"She oughta know!" Miss Spindler seemed to know everything there was to know in the neighborhood, usually before it even happened. Now that I knew how she kept up on all of us in SummerHill, I didn't pursue things with Mom. I'd play it safe and keep quiet.

"Is it classified information that's keeping you so busy over at our Amish neighbors' farm?" Mom asked gently—not probing, really, just terribly interested.

"I'm helping Rachel care for one of the new lambs."

"Oh?"

"The lamb's sickly . . . an orphan. She won't take to the bottle very well."

Mom's eyes were wide. "How very sad."

"That's why I'm going over there so much."

Mom nodded her head, taking a deep breath. "Well, I'm glad to know this isn't about Rachel's brother."

"Oh, Mom," I laughed it off, "you can relax about Levi. He has a new girlfriend, I'm pretty sure."

Our conversation ended quickly enough, but another was soon to take place. The prelude to it occurred when I bumped in to Dad on my way past his study.

"Hi, Dad," I said, glad to see him. "What have you been doing all day?" I followed him up the steps.

"I think it's time to finish our talk," he said. "I'll meet you in the backyard at the gazebo in, say, ten minutes?"

I checked my watch. "Sure, but first I have to make a phone call."

He smiled faintly, and I hurried to my brother's

room, where I dialed Jon Klein. "Hi, Jon," I said when he answered. "It's me, Merry."

"Hey!" He was truly glad to hear from me. "I hope you're coming tomorrow."

"I'd really like to, but I promised to help Rachel Zook after school."

"Oh." A weighty silence followed. He probably wanted an explanation and deserved one. But how could I tell him I was choosing a sick and possibly neurotic animal over him? I couldn't. He might not understand, and I didn't want to risk losing my friendship with him. Besides, I could feel it in my bones—I was getting closer to a breakthrough with little Jingle Belle.

"Maybe I'll go the next time," I spoke up.

"How about next week?" he persisted.

"Why, what's happening then?"

"Some kids from my photography class are going down to the banks of the Susquehanna River. We'll shoot a roll of film, walk along the river . . . just immerse ourselves in the surroundings."

"Church friends?" I asked, knowing how picky Dad was.

"Two are." The others were school friends of Jon's. But I didn't know them.

I was pretty sure Dad would say I couldn't go. "I guess not. And I'm sorry about tomorrow."

"Will you let me know sooner . . . next time?"
He sounded annoyed.

"Yeah, I can do that." Truth was, I could've let
him know *this* time but didn't. I'd treated his invi-
tation with reckless indifference.

Again, we hung up on a slightly sour note. I truly
hoped Jon would understand about Rachel's lamb
once I told him the whole story. If he'd just be patient long enough.

❦   ❦

By the time I met Dad at the gazebo, he was
looking out through the white latticework. "What
took you so long?" he joked.

"Jonathan Klein."

"Great kid . . . I like him." Dad was grinning
now, raising his eyebrows at me.

"He seems to like you, too," I said, eager to know
what was on his mind. "So what are we talking
about?"

"Your mother," he said.

My breath caught in my throat. "She's not sick,
is she?" Illness was always the first thought to come
to mind. Because of Faithie.

He shook his head, turning to lean against the
wood railing so that he was now facing me. "Your
mom's going through what's commonly known as a

40

midlife crisis, although *I* don't think it's anything to worry about." He paused, raking his fingers through his hair. "I think her antique shop idea is an excellent one. It'll keep her busy."

"Is there anything I can do? I mean, to make Mom feel better?"

"Maybe there is," he said more softly. "Why don't you talk to her . . . about Faithie. Share your memories of your twin sister."

"Would she want to? I mean, are you sure about this?"

He nodded, eyes glistening. "Mom still misses Faith terribly. We all do."

"We all do. . . ." His words tumbled over and over in my brain.

I don't honestly know how I got from where I was standing across the gazebo to my father's arms. Somehow, I managed through a mist of tears. Dad wrapped me in his strong embrace, and I smelled his subtle cologne fragrance and felt the texture of his golf shirt on my cheek. "Oh, Daddy," I cried. "I miss Faithie, too."

FIVE

I would've offered to ride along with Mom after school the next day. I had actually planned to go antique browsing with her, but Rachel Zook was sitting on the white gazebo steps when I came bounding up the back walk. Wisps of her light brown hair had slipped out from under her head covering. It looked like she'd run all the way through the willow grove to get here.

"Hi, Rachel," I said, observing her black dress and gray apron. Looked like Amish mourning clothes to me. "Jingle didn't die, did she?" I barely got the words out.

"No . . . no, no," she said, glancing down at her drab clothing. "But I don't blame ya for thinkin' that." Her face broke into a broad smile. "But Jingle's still only takin' enough nourishment to keep her alive. Dat's got her on tube-feeding now."

The muscles in my jaw began to relax. "You had me worried for a minute."

"Jah, I 'spect I did."

I invited her inside for lemonade and freshly baked cookies. I just assumed there would be some ready and waiting on the kitchen counter, because that was Mom's usual after-school snack for me in the spring and summer.

We weren't disappointed. Mom had gone the extra mile and not only made oatmeal cookies but an apple crumb cake, too, along with a pitcher filled with sweet lemonade.

"Your mom's an awful gut cook," Rachel said, sitting down at the table with me.

"That's a compliment, coming from you," I replied, knowing what an incredible cook *her* mother was.

Then, out of the blue, Rachel said, "Jingle's bein' shunned by the flock."

I sat up straight in my chair. "Why, what's happened?"

"It's the same as before. The rest of the sheep sense her troubled state."

"Maybe you should keep force-feeding her," I suggested.

Rachel shook her head. "Dat and Mam think it's

just a matter of days and she'll be gone. Unless . . ." Her voice faded away.

"Unless what?"

"Well, if it ain't God's will for her to go just yet."

I should've known Rachel would say that. God's sovereign will covered all His creation. I just hadn't thought to invite the Lord into the situation. "Let's ask God to help us with Jingle," I said, ready to pray right then.

She didn't answer, but her blue eyes were serious. "Talkin' like that to God is up to you . . . and Levi," she said softly.

"Levi?" I was startled to hear her mention his name.

"He's home for a visit. Arrived not more than an hour ago."

So Miss Spindler was right. Once again, she knew what she was talking about. "Has Levi prayed for the lamb yet?" I asked.

"Not that I know of, but he's looked her over real gut. 'Tween you and me, I doubt he's as concerned 'bout Jingle as we are."

"What do you mean?"

Her eyes took on an almost distant look. "S'posin' his distraction is understandable."

I listened, waiting for more.

"Levi brought a girl home . . . to meet us,"

Rachel sputtered out the words.

"His girlfriend from the Mennonite college?"

"Jah."

So I was right all these weeks about my suspicions. No wonder his letters had stopped. Quickly, I remembered my manners. "Well, I'm happy for him. For you, too, Rachel."

"Me?" Rachel blinked her eyes. "Don'tcha know, I was hopin' *you'd* be my sister-in-law someday, Cousin Merry."

I laughed softly. "Oh, things are over between Levi and me. He's all grown-up now, and a Mennonite, too. I never would've fit very well in his Plain world."

"I s'pose not," she whispered, head down. "But it was awful nice to hope."

Getting up, I carried the pitcher of lemonade to the table. "You know, I just realized Levi hasn't heard the news about Miss Spindler's secret."

"Don'tcha mean Old Hawk Eyes?" Rachel asked.

"She's just Miss Spindler now. I don't think she deserves a nickname anymore. Never did, really." Miss Spindler had turned out to be a remarkably astute old lady. Outsmarting all of us.

"I'm sure Levi's gonna want to see you while he's home," Rachel said before she left.

My heart actually stayed put hearing that. I guess I surprised myself, too. Maybe I was truly over my romantic interest in my lifelong friend. "I'd like to meet his girlfriend sometime," I told her.

"You mean you'd like to *approve* of her?"

We literally howled at that, and since parting for us was always next to impossible, I walked all the way out to the lane and down to the willow grove shortcut with her.

The branches above us mushroomed over our heads like a giant tent. Deep in the willows, we found our secret place, more beautiful than one could imagine. The place had belonged to Faithie and me first. After her death, Rachel and I had claimed it as our own. Only one adult had ever visited here. My mother. That was a little over a year ago, the day I'd discovered baby Charity abandoned in our gazebo.

Beyond the willow grove was pure sunshine. Only a few shadows here and there. Golden rays bounced off the grassy meadow to the west of the Zooks' barnyard. And out behind the barn, the pond was aglow with dancing light. Summer was almost here!

Rachel told me about the baptism classes she was taking, along with Matthew Yoder. "I believe I'm ready to join the Amish church, Merry."

"You sure?"

"Jah, it's the right way for me," she said reverently. "Matthew and I will both take our kneelin' vow come this September."

"I'm not surprised."

She smiled, her dimples showing. "A gut many young people will be joining church this fall. Oh my, and Dat's ever so glad 'bout it."

I thought of Abe Zook's disappointment over his second son, Levi, joining ranks with the Mennonites. "Makes up for certain ones *not* joining, I guess."

"Jah, and Dat thinks it's high time we take back our children from the clutches of the world," Rachel said unexpectedly. "He's started speakin' out more and more 'bout raising the standard for our young people."

"Does he plan to talk to Levi about returning to his Amish roots?"

"Well, yes and no. It's a right touchy situation, with Martha around and all."

"Martha?"

"Levi's girlfriend—Martha Martin."

For a second, I nearly laughed, thinking of the alliteration. "Is she staying at your house?" I asked, composing myself.

She nodded sheepishly. "I'm sharing my room with her."

"You'll get acquainted real quick that way."

"Well, ain't that the truth!"

I watched her turn and head out of the willow grove, her slender form flitting through the trees and the underbrush as the sun twinkled down on her.

"I'll be right over after I change clothes," I hollered to her, remembering the dear little lamb who needed me.

"Make it snappy!" she called over her shoulder.

I would hurry, all right. Because I was sure I knew what to do to get Jingle's attention. I could hardly wait to try!

On the way back up the hill, I saw Mom driving out of our lane, then make the turn onto Strawberry Lane. Where was she headed? She never went into town that way. It was the opposite direction!

Quickening my pace, I shot through the front and side yards. Just in time, too, because when I peered through the trees, I saw Mom pulling into our neighbor's driveway. "What's she doing at Miss Spindler's?" I wondered aloud.

Mom and Ruby Spindler had been casual friends for as long as I remembered. Our elderly neighbor seemed to enjoy doting on our family, sharing her freshly baked pies and other pastries. But never had she and Mom been close friends. So this was a surprise! In fact, if I hadn't had an ailing lamb to tend to, I would've schemed to get to the bottom of Mom's visit with our eccentric neighbor. But I had more important things on my mind. Today, I intended to change the course of Jingle Belle's life!

SIX

The afternoon sky had begun to turn overcast by the time I changed clothes and headed toward the Zooks' farm. Because of the gray clouds, I felt somewhat gloomy. But I was determined to help Jingle Belle, so I tried to ignore the discouraged feeling.

When I saw Rachel, I told her only a select part of my idea. "I've been thinking of doing something. It might sound a little weird. But . . . it just might save Jingle's life."

She gave me a sidelong glance, but I ignored it. We waited near the fence for the orphaned lamb to wander over. The tiny bell tinkled its sweet sound, and we petted Jingle's soft coat.

A lump caught in my throat when I saw how pitiful she was. Like a shadow of herself. "She's pining away, all right," I whispered.

"An awful shame," Rachel replied softly.

I considered my unconventional idea, pondering it over and over in my mind. Then I got brave and made my intention known, so I wouldn't get cold feet and back out. "Do you think it's safe for me to go inside the fence?" I asked Rachel at last.

"Well, Merry, whatever for?"

"I want to try to enter Jingle's world, so to speak. Honestly, I think she'll take the nursing bottle better if I do."

"I just don't know . . ."

"Isn't it worth a try?" I insisted.

Rachel scanned the area, shading her eyes with one hand. "Ach, just a minute! Looks to me like Dat and Levi let the rams out to the back pasture." It was true, only the ewes and smaller sheep—and Jingle Belle—remained in the enclosure. "It *might* well be safe enough for ya," she said, still surveying things.

"Maybe this is providential," I spoke up. "With the rams let out and all."

Rachel seemed to like my mention of "providential." Delight was written on her face. "Jah, maybe it's not such a bad idea, after all." And she ran to get the bottle of milk.

While she was gone, I prayed that God would help me connect with the starving lamb. "Somehow, Lord, please let Jingle take more nourishment

52

today," I prayed under my breath. "Please . . ."

My eyes caught sight of the willow tree, the one that had grown from a simple fishing pole. *If Faithie were alive, she'd be right here, helping me,* I thought. But I knew better than to talk to my sister who'd gone to heaven. It was God who would help me now.

"Here you are," Rachel said, running toward me with the bottle of milk.

I tested the nipple, squirting a thin stream of milk on Jingle's nose by accident. Then I climbed over the plank fence. "Hello, sweet girl," I whispered, sitting down next to Jingle. "I'm here, baby, just for you."

She began to nuzzle next to me, making the saddest, yet dearest sounds. Jingle Belle was crying. Someone had cared enough to crawl over the fence. To *her* side!

Almost at once, the clouds seemed to part, allowing the sun to break through for a moment. When I offered the milk bottle, there was no hesitation from Jingle. The lamb drank heartily.

"That-a girl," I whispered, holding hard to the bottle.

Rachel was nearly breathless with excitement. "Wait'll I tell Dat and Mam," I heard her say, and then she flew off toward the house.

"You're the best little lamb I know," I cooed to

Jingle, who didn't seem to mind my dinner talk. "We'll fatten you up and get you well, don't you worry."

There were only the contented sounds of Jingle's suckle. No sorrowful murmurings. I was overjoyed! "Thank you, Lord" was all I could say.

By the time Rachel arrived, bringing along her mother, Esther Zook, and the rest of the children, Jingle had come close to draining the bottle dry.

"Let's get her more milk!" young Nancy exclaimed.

"Jah, and hurry up about it," Mrs. Zook said, clapping her hands.

The second bottle disappeared almost as quickly, and Jingle began to nod her head up and down. "Look, she's thankin' you, Merry," little Susie said.

I climbed out of the fence and stood there with the Zooks, admiring the lamb on the other side.

"I should say, I believe she's gonna live," Esther announced under a bluer sky than before. "Well, I do declare."

"Wait'll we tell Levi," said Nancy and Ella Mae.

"Praise be!" little Susie said, and the younger girls scampered off.

"We're ever so grateful to you," Rachel said, throwing her arms around me in a jubilant hug.

"I'm just glad it turned out this way," I said.

" 'Merry had a little lamb, it's fleece was white as snow,' " Rachel's mother recited comically.

Rachel herself finished the verse. " 'And everywhere that Merry went, the lamb was sure to go.' "

We had a good laugh, but there was more to it. A precious animal's life had been saved. Right before our eyes!

❧   ❧

Later that night, as I dressed for bed, I thought of Jingle and her world of the sheep corral. What had made me think to crawl over the fence and join her there? More than that, why had it worked?

The night sky was evident through the curtains. White fog had begun to descend on Lancaster County. I went to stand at one of the windows, looking out at the ancient maple in our front yard. Far sturdier than the frail weeping willow near the sheep fence, this tree had shaded our lawn for more than a hundred and fifty years, providing refuge on hot days and lending support for a wooden swing, too. It was also the tree Lissa Vyner, my dear friend, had crouched under, calling me out of bed one moonlit night nearly two years ago. I hadn't know it then, but along the way—since that night—God had made me aware of my "helping" gift. First stray cats, then an abused girl friend, an autistic boy, an abandoned baby, and now a sickly lamb.

Often, I worried that I got too caught up in my "Miss Fix-It" mentality. But I'm coming to understand myself better these days. I'm not so hard on myself, I guess. Losing Faithie may have gotten the helper thing going. I don't know for sure. It really doesn't matter. What counts is that I'm depending on the Lord for heavenly help.

Before slipping into bed, I thanked God again for letting Jingle live. "That dear little lamb is a lot like I was after Faithie died. For years, I couldn't cry over her. Remember, Lord? But when I finally did, I started to heal."

I brushed my tears away. "I think when Jingle drank all that milk today, she began to heal, too," I continued my prayer. "Thank you, God, for giving me the idea about going into *her* world . . . the way Jesus did for us when He left heaven and came to earth."

I hadn't thought of the connection before— between what God did for humanity and what I'd done for Jingle—but it got me wound up. I really couldn't sleep a wink, I was that excited.

Instead of wasting time tossing in bed, I got up and went to my desk and turned on the light. Now was a good time to double-check my English assignment for tomorrow, and while I was at it, I scrutinized my math and history homework, too.

I thought of my school and church friends: Lissa Vyner, Chelsea Davis, and Ashley Horton. All three would be giggling if they could see me now.

It turned out that I only stayed up till just past eleven. Soon, I fell into a delicious, deep sleep. I dreamed I was a tall, sturdy maple tree, planted near a river. Like the one in the first psalm. My roots reached far down into the soil, and nothing could shake me.

When I awakened hours later, my arms were stiff and nearly numb, like frozen tree branches in winter. I sat up in bed, moving my arms to get the blood circulating. Yet the tree dream lingered in my mind, the most peculiar dream ever.

SEVEN

The rain stopped sometime in the wee hours, Mom told me at breakfast. And the ominous white fog dissipated by the time I left the house to stand along SummerHill Lane, waiting for the school bus. I had a good feeling that this was going to be a beautiful day.

To start with, Jon saved a place for me on the bus next to him. Chelsea, in her regular spot, sat across the aisle from us, her nose in a book. She looked up briefly when I got on, pushed her thick auburn locks behind one ear, then flipped back through the pages in her book.

"What's she reading?" I asked Jon, smiling at him.

"Must be something very deep" came his answer, far less ecstatic than usual.

I knew why. I'd hurt Jon by not going on the hike with him. Taking a deep breath, I made an attempt at smoothing things over. "I'm really sorry about yesterday," I managed, but my words came out flat.

"The hike?" He shrugged. "Forget it."

I didn't dare ask if he had a good time, or even if he went at all. The thought crossed my mind that he might've wanted to ask someone else, since I didn't go. It wasn't as if he and I were in an exclusive dating relationship or anything. My parents would never allow such a thing. Not at *my* age—going on fifteen.

We rode in silence all the way to school. I stared straight ahead, looking out the wide dash window up front, feeling very awkward about the tension between Jon and me.

When we arrived, I could hardly wait to get off the bus. I scurried to the shelter of my locker without another word to Jon.

Chelsea followed close behind. "You two aren't exactly humming today. Is it because you stood him up?"

"Chelsea Davis, I did *not!*"

"Well, what do you call it?" Her green eyes flashed.

I was no dummy. She'd definitely heard *someone's*

60

version of the story. I wondered how many other girls Jon had told.

"You stood him up," Chelsea accused me again.

"I'm late for homeroom," I blurted.

"We just got here, remember?"

"I must be late for something." I reached for my three-ring binder, and a landslide of books followed behind. "Yee-ikes! Look what you made me do!" I hollered, causing students to gawk.

"I'm outa here," she said, launching into the tidal wave of humanity in the hallway.

I fumed, wishing Chelsea hadn't said what she'd said. Wishing, too, I hadn't retaliated and treated her truly horribly. I gathered my books and stuffed them back in my locker. I wished something else, too—that I had been completely honest with Jon. What on earth had kept me from telling him about Rachel's lamb? Why was I protecting my experience with a helpless animal, keeping it from a close friend like Jon?

I don't know how long I stood there, staring and fuming into my locker. It must've been long enough to lose myself in my anger, because, suddenly, I heard a voice behind me.

"What're you doing, Mer?"

Turning around, I saw Lissa Vyner frowning at me. "Hey, what's up, Liss?"

"Asked you first."

I sighed. "Whatever."

"So?" I figured she wouldn't leave me alone till I spilled out my problems to her. Lissa was like that—she could pretty much read my facial expressions and know when I was really upset.

"I was a jerk to Chelsea," I admitted.

"No kidding. News like that travels with the speed of sound." She nodded solemnly. "It's not like you, Merry," she said softly.

"I know, and I'm sorry. It's just that . . ."

"Is it about you and Jon?" she asked.

I couldn't bear to hear any of this. Not from meek and mild Lissa. "Who all knows about this, for Pete's sake?"

She shrugged, taking a step closer to me. "Jon thinks you like Levi Zook *again*. He thinks that's why you're spending so much time at the Amish farm."

I shook my head. "I haven't even seen Levi."

"Then he *is* back?" Her eyes were wider than I'd seen them in a long time.

"His sister said he was visiting, and I heard he was working with his dad, but, honestly, I have *not* seen him." I paused, closing my locker. "Please tell Jon that Levi and I are ancient history!"

She smiled, hugging me. "That's all I wanted to hear."

The first-period bell rang, and we parted ways.
No wonder Jon was so quiet on the bus, I thought.
He was freaked over Levi's return. But Jon had nothing to fear. Levi had a college girlfriend now. He was in love with someone new.

Then I felt it, my first twinge of uncertainty. It definitely wasn't jealousy or anything like that. I slid into my homeroom desk and glanced at my assignment notebook. Browsing through my schedule for the day, I realized the twinge had become more of a stabbing pain. I could never, ever reveal this to my girl friends. And I would keep it secret from Jon, too. No one needed to know. Because this was totally absurd.

Yet the more I thought of Levi in love with Martha Martin, whoever she was, the more I cringed. My toes even curled up inside my tennies, and I felt the tension in my jaw. But I had no choice—I'd just have to deal with it. Besides, it was too late now; I'd stuck my neck out, for sure. Why had I told Rachel I wanted to meet Levi's girlfriend?

What *was* I thinking?

I groaned so loudly, several students turned around and glared at me. Sadly for me, the day was turning out to be less than beautiful.

EIGHT

The house was filled with music when I arrived home. The CD player was blaring with the likes of Mozart and Haydn. The cats didn't seem to mind the classical racket. Actually, they were busy scarfing down their usual afternoon snack.

"What's with the music?" I asked, giving Mom a quick hug.

"I'm attempting to raise the cats' level of intelligence." Her eyes twinkled.

"By playing the classics?" This was just too weird.

"I read that it works for human babies, so why not cats?"

"You can't be serious," I said, getting down on the floor to pet my favorite kitties.

"Oh yes, I am." She carried a plate of warm

cookies to the kitchen table. "And . . . I'm practicing my ability to soothe customers while I'm at it."

I looked up from my vantage point on the floor. Mom was absolutely radiant. She didn't seem in need of a heart-to-heart talk, like Dad had said. Maybe he was mistaken. On second thought, maybe he was right. Maybe Mom was submerging her sorrow in planning a business.

"Miss Spindler's agreed to be my partner. She and I have already discussed things, and we're definitely having soft music piped into our little antique shop."

"Dad told me you wanted to fix up the shed—start an antique business."

She nodded. "Yes, and I've already begun to sort through old things, mostly junk that can be hauled away."

"Are you actually going to do this?"

"Oh, Merry, honey, I'm so excited!" She gave me an impulsive hug.

"Did Dad mention the possibility of tourists trampling your flower beds?" I couldn't see how any of this was a good idea.

"Oh, nonsense," and she waved her hand as if tourists were not a concern. "The stone walkway will lead right to the shop. No trampling worries."

I was surprised at her response. "Better ask

Rachel and her mother about some of the rude folks they've encountered."

But Mom was insistent. She was determined to open a cozy shop in the backyard. She was going to focus on antiques—the past—in order to handle the present. And possibly her future, too: life minus Faithie. I was convinced more than ever that losing Faithie was behind all this talk.

⚘　⚘

I finished my homework in record time. Two hours. Then I called Chelsea. My lousy behavior had begun to gnaw away at my conscience. I wanted to apologize for my outburst at school. But she wasn't at home, so I called Lissa. "Any idea where Chelsea is?" I asked.

"How should I know?"

"She's gotta be around SummerHill some-where," I mumbled into the phone. It made no sense for me to ask Lissa where Chelsea was because Chelsea Davis lived up the hill from *me*. And Lissa lived miles away.

"Why don't you just call Jon?" Lissa suggested. "That's who you *really* want to talk to, right?"

Lissa knew me well. I smiled into the phone. "I just don't know what to say to him. He wasn't very talkative on the bus today . . . morning or after-noon."

"Start with Levi Zook. Get it out in the open. Let Jon hear it from you that Levi's out of the picture."

"I thought you told Jon in study hall," I said.

"Sure, but—"

"What did Jon say?"

Lissa sighed into the phone. "To tell you the truth, Mer, he just nodded his head."

"Like he didn't believe you?"

"You could say that." She paused, then continued. "I really think you should call Jon."

I was surprised at Lissa's persistence. This was very different for her. "Okay, I will . . . later. Right now I've got something important to do."

"More important than your *boyfriend*? I can't believe this. What could be so important?" She really wanted to know, but I wasn't telling. "I thought we were superclose, Mer," she said, sounding less confident.

"We are," I assured her. "Lighten up, Lissa."

She was silent for a moment, then giggled a little. "Did you just say what I think you said?"

"Yeah. So?"

"But you quit the Alliteration Game, right?"

"Yeah, I quit."

"Except you just did it . . . again."

She was right. "Oh, that. Well, for some reason it seems to fly out of my mouth automatically every now and then."

"Maybe that's because it's a part of who you are after all this time."

Funny how Lissa's comment fit right into what I'd been thinking about Levi Zook.

After all this time . . .

Levi was a big part of my life, too. How could I let him slip out of it, smack dab into Martha's?

I could hear Lissa's mom calling her in the background, so we said good-bye and hung up. I was glad our conversation ended with Lissa's explanation of why she thought I was still alliterating my words. Much better than pleading with me for answers. I hadn't told her the cool thing Jon had said not too long ago. *"You're the Queen of Alliteration,"* he'd announced one day. Where that particular thought came from, I didn't know. Anyway, it was little consolation at the moment.

Fact was, both Jon and Levi had been a huge part of my life. And for a very long time. Levi and I, however, went back a few years further than Jon and I. Still, it was terribly unnerving to care so much for two boys. At the same time!

69

Rachel Zook came over before supper. "Jingle won't take the bottle from any of us," Rachel said, her blue eyes earnest as can be. "She needs you, Merry."

"I'm coming," I said, then called to Mom over my shoulder. "I'll be back in an hour or so."

"Where are you going?" she said, coming into the kitchen.

"I'm 'on call' at the Zook farm," I told her, laughing.

The air was as sweet and clean as fresh laundry hung out to dry. And as Rachel and I ran through the yard to SummerHill Lane and then into the willow grove, a peculiar thought hit me. What would Mom do about her clothesline if customers were coming and going at her antique shop? Would she give up one of life's simple pleasures to accommodate shoppers? I couldn't imagine her dumping clothes into an electric dryer, except during inclement weather. I made a mental note to ask her.

"Something on your mind?" Rachel asked halfway through the abundant thicket of willow trees and vegetation.

"Oh, it's my mother. She's having some sort of a midlife crisis."

"What's *that*?"

"Well, she's almost fifty. Thinks life is passing

her by, I guess. That's how my dad explained it."

"*My* mother's older than that." Rachel slowed her pace to a stroll. We walked single file down past the tallest trees, then turned toward the meadow that led to the Zooks' barnyard. "Never heard of such a thing, really," Rachel said. "Maybe it's something *Englischers* get."

"You're probably right," I said with a chuckle. Middle-aged Amish folk didn't have time to feel sorry about their children growing up and going to college. They were too busy raising the tail end of a long line of children. No empty-nest syndrome till the grandchildren started coming on. Besides that, most of their young people never went off to college because the bishops didn't allow education past the eighth grade. A Plain wife didn't have to worry about early retirement for her husband. Amish farmers, carpenters, and blacksmiths worked up until God called them home. Or until they couldn't physically work any longer. That's the way it was in the Anabaptist community.

"Is your mother gonna be all right?" asked Rachel. "Is she seein' a doctor?"

I stifled a laugh. "It's not as serious as that. Mom's going to start up an antique shop in our backyard. It'll give her something to keep her mind off herself."

"That doesn't sound so bad," Rachel replied, looking more confused than before. "Maybe I can help tend the store sometimes."

Leave it to Rachel to offer. "I'm sure Mom would love to have some expert help."

"Expert?"

"Well, you know, all the experience you have from your fruit and vegetable stands."

"Oh, I see what you're sayin'."

We climbed over the fence that divided the open pastureland from the side yard. That's when I spied a Mennonite girl hanging out clothes on the line behind the Zooks' farmhouse. "Is that Levi's girlfriend?" I whispered.

"Jah," answered Rachel. "Come, I'll introduce you."

I felt myself holding back, feeling suddenly shy. I wasn't sure why, but I put on a smile. "Sure, that'd be nice," I said, following Rachel to the wide backyard.

We walked right up to the clothesline. The young woman was clearly a strict Mennonite. The hem of her floral print dress came well below her knees. Her hair was a lighter brown than Rachel's, more like the color of ripened wheat. And her bright brown eyes—you couldn't help but notice the sparkle.

"Martha, I want you to meet my friend Merry

Hanson," said Rachel. "Merry lives past the willow grove across the way." She pointed toward my house, to the west, then turned to me. "And, Merry, this is Martha Martin from the Mennonite college in Virginia, where Levi goes to school."

"Hello, Merry," Martha Martin said, extending her hand.

"Nice to meet you," I said, wondering why Rachel hadn't just said Martha was Levi's girlfriend.

"SummerHill is a beautiful place," Martha was saying. Her smile was contagious. Actually, everything about her was delightful. I could see why Levi had fallen in love. "How long have you lived here, Merry?" she asked.

"My whole life, pretty much."

"Then you've been friends with Rachel for a long time?"

I glanced at Rachel, who was nodding and grinning at me. "Since we were toddlers, I guess you could say."

Rachel spoke up. "All us kids were good friends with Merry and her brother, Skip."

"And Faithie, too," I added.

Rachel's eyes softened, and she tilted her head against the sun. "Faithie was Merry's twin sister," she said softly.

It was so uncanny, because Martha really didn't

have to be told that Faithie had died. I guess the way Rachel said "Faithie *was* Merry's twin sister" gave it away.

"I'm sorry about your sister," Martha replied. She was so sweet and gentle-spirited. As much as I might've wanted to be upset with her for latching on to Levi, I simply couldn't be. She was the perfect choice for a former Amish boy called into the ministry.

After I gave Jingle her nursing bottle—and she drank every drop—I headed home, alone. This time, I stopped in the middle of the willow grove and sat on a dead tree stump in the secret place. I thought about meeting Martha Martin, the amazing Mennonite maid.

When I saw Levi again, I would tell him what a wonderful girl she was. I would congratulate him, too.

It was really the weirdest thing, but my twinges and stabs were actually starting to go away. How could I be so back and forth about things?

NINE

I caught up with Chelsea at Wednesday night Bible study, before church in the girls' rest room. "I tried to call you after school," I said.

She didn't bother to turn away from the mirror, but our eyes caught all the same.

"Look, I don't blame you for being upset," I continued. "I shouldn't have freaked out like that."

"No kidding," she muttered.

"I'm sorry, Chelsea. It won't happen again."
She smirked.

Several girls and their mother came in just then. I knew we'd have to finish the one-sided conversation later. Anyway, it was obvious Chelsea wasn't in the mood to forgive me any time soon.

"Can we talk later?" I said softly.

She acted as if she hadn't heard me, same as before.

"Chelsea?"

She turned and glared at me. "Tomorrow," she whispered and left.

I washed my hands without ever looking in the mirror.

❧ ❧

It was late in the day when I went outside in my pajamas and looked up at the sky. Shadrach and Meshach had followed me. I knew it wouldn't be long before the other cats would come, too. It was almost completely dark as I sat on the back steps, thinking about what the future held for me. For my friends, too.

Rachel and Matthew Yoder were following the traditional Amish courting rituals. I was pretty sure they'd marry a full year from now, come November. Levi and Martha Martin were probably headed in the same matrimonial direction.

Stars were beginning to appear, one at a time, like city lights. Cicadas and crickets began singing their night songs, calling back and forth. First in one clump of bushes, then another group joined in, until an entire choir of nighttime insects' sounds mingled with the dark blue dusk.

Would I be sitting here if Faithie were alive tonight? I asked myself. *Would I be contemplating my future?*

76

I pictured the two of us sitting on the steps, pointing out one star after another, maybe even spotting a planet or two. She would be wearing different pajamas than mine, though. Even as a little girl, she'd had strong opinions about us not looking exactly alike—doing our hair different, wearing distinct outfits. I was pretty sure, though, that we'd be barefoot if we were here together. Letting the cool green grass tickle our feet was something we always liked to do in the evening hours when the day was dying down. And she would've liked cuddling up with the cats. As for her taking in strays, I doubt it.

If Faithie had continued as she was—much more like Mom—she probably would've shied away from having so many pets. She might've turned out to be intolerant toward my cats, the way Mom often was. Then again, maybe I wouldn't have needed so many cats, or any at all, if Faithie had lived.

"Oh, Lord, I wish I could get past the hurdle of my sister's death. It's like a shadow shrouding the gateway to my future."

I thought of Jingle Belle, how she would only take her milk when I held the nursing bottle. What did it mean? Could she sense my great personal loss?

Sitting outside under the vast sky, it was easy to feel sorry for myself, being the surviving twin. I often wondered why God hadn't let Faithie live instead of me. Why *not* her? Was it because she was born first—twenty minutes before me? She always had to be the first to show Mom and Dad her report card, first to wrap her Christmas presents, and first in most any footrace. Did she have to outdistance me and beat me to heaven, too?

I leaned back on my elbows, staring hard at the sky. It was turning slate gray, and the stars seemed brighter than before. In the stillness, I wondered what the insects were saying to each other. Were they calling back and forth, "We can sing louder than you"? "No, *we* can . . . we can . . ." Were they debating the time of tomorrow's sunrise?

Sighing, I listened till the choristers blended into one clamorous cadenza. The half-moon surprised me when it appeared, floating up over the trees, its light clinging to the east side of the gazebo. A lonely owl hooted into the chaos of the night chorus, and I felt a slight chill.

One thing I knew for sure: Rachel's lamb had stirred up everything about Faithie's death. Jingle and I had connected somehow. We were linked with a common cord. And God had answered my prayer for the sick little animal.

I sighed, looking down as I felt two furry bodies pushing into my lap. Just as I thought, Abednego and Lily White had made their presence known.

They didn't want to miss out on getting attention.

"Where have you been?" I asked, petting them both. "Did you think I'd gone and left you?"

Mew. Abednego had the audacity!

"Don't you know I'd never do that," I insisted. "You can count on me!"

"I will not leave you comfortless . . ." The verse in John's gospel popped into my mind. It had been one of the Scripture readings at Faithie's funeral. Our pastor had said God would never abandon us in our sorrow. He would take care of us in our loneliness, in our sadness.

"God cares more about me than I care for my cats," I said aloud, surprising myself.

God cares . . .

I stayed outside another fifteen minutes or so, letting the truth sink in. The insects had calmed down. I hadn't been aware of the silence until now. No more competitive chirping and singing back and forth between bushes.

The moon's light had shifted. Now it lay across the back steps, where I was surrounded by cats. The beauty of the night and the stillness made me feel like crying. The tears came for all the days and nights I had missed Faithie. All the life experiences we might've shared together.

I wiped my nose on the hem of my pajama top,

something my twin would *never* have done. Realizing that, I began to snicker.

Getting up, I opened the door and headed back into the house. Without saying good-night to either of my parents, I made a beeline to my room and fell on my knees beside my bed.

Would God answer my prayer and lift my burden? Was it too much to ask?

TEN

I should've known Mom would have a hefty breakfast spread out when I came downstairs. Several days had passed since she'd last made waffles. Scrambled eggs, bacon, and jelly toast were her usual fare, even when things were rushed. But today it was the works, and I reminded her that it was just Thursday. "Not Saturday brunch."

"It's your next-to-last week of school before summer vacation," she said, which made absolutely no sense to me. "You need a good breakfast to keep you going."

"I don't get it, Mom. You don't have to knock yourself out making all this food. It's just breakfast, for Pete's sake."

She ignored my comments and set about pouring orange juice in her best juice glasses. "Your father and I are going to Bird-in-Hand to talk to a Mennonite antique dealer today."

"Have fun," I said offhandedly.

Mom must've picked up on the tone of my remark. She turned, and then I noticed she was still wearing her bathrobe. "What's the matter, Merry?" she asked.

Since Mom hardly ever wore her bathrobe downstairs, I guess I might've been staring at her. "What . . . what did you say?"

"The antique business," she stated. "You seem opposed to the idea."

"Oh, I don't really care," I answered, wondering how I should proceed. "I guess it's not the coolest thing, dealing in ancient history. That's all."

Mom sat across the table from me. Her face was crestfallen. "Merry, honey, I'd like to say something."

I nodded, feeling lousy now. Dad had asked me to please reach out to Mom, not alienate her with flippant remarks.

She sighed audibly. "You may not realize this, but I happen to like the idea of selling antiques. It's one of my goals . . . something I've wanted to do for a very long time."

"Since Skip went to college?" I asked, hoping it was the right thing to say.

82

"Long before that," she replied, pushing her hair behind her ear. "I'd say I've wanted to do the antique thing ever since you and Faithie were born."

Faithie . . .

So I was right.

"Authentic antiques have a unique quality." She paused, smiling faintly. "I feel renewed when I'm surrounded by the past."

"Old things won't bring Faithie back," I said softly.

Her eyes widened, her forehead creased into a deep frown. "Excuse me?"

I shook my head. "Oh, nothing."

"No . . . you said something quite startling, Merry. I think we should talk about this."

Glancing at my watch, I saw that we didn't have time for a knock-down, drag-out conversation. Unfortunately, I had a desperate feeling that's what it might turn out to be. "Can it wait till after school?"

We both heard Dad's footsteps at the same time. "Perhaps," she said, sounding worse than forlorn. She was heartbroken. Thanks to me.

Once again, I'd made a fatal error. First Chelsea, now Mom. "I'm sorry," I managed to say before Dad came in and sat down. He reached for the newspaper and opened it, which was a good thing. For now, he wouldn't see the sadness in Mom's eyes.

I, on the other hand, observed her grief all too well.

❧　❧

To top things off, Chelsea was sitting next to Jon when I boarded the bus. They were having a lively conversation, so I walked past them and sat farther back, where I could observe them in private. I had no idea what was going on. But Chelsea was up to something—I could count on it!

Several times during the ride to school, Jon glanced back at me. I managed to divert my eyes so that he wouldn't think I was watching them. It had nothing to do with jealousy because I knew Chelsea had no interest in Jon Klein. And even if she had, I knew perfectly well how Jon felt about me. He and I had been good friends since our primary grades in elementary school, and only recently had we decided to "go out."

Chelsea actually waited for me to get off the bus. "Can we talk now?" *She* was asking me! She fell into step with me, and I kept my eye on Jon as he hurried into the school ahead of us. "I'll be straight with you, Merry," she began.

"What?"

"You've got plenty of competition, in case you don't know."

84

"What're you talking about?" I said.

"Jon wants to know why you stood him up for the hike."

I felt the same resentment as yesterday when she accused me of the same thing. "I told you, I didn't stand him up."

She waved her hand. "Call it what you like. Truth is, you've been ignoring him."

"Why should *you* care?"

"Jonathan's my friend," she replied. "I'm not going to stand by and watch you hurt him."

I had no idea where she was going with this. "Jon and I will work it out," I told her. "Stay out of it."

She gave me a severe frown and flounced off.

Immediately, I headed for Jon's locker. Before I could think twice and chicken out, I walked right up to him and said, "I don't think it's fair what you're saying about me."

He turned to look at me, his brown eyes thoughtful. His shirt was a soft yellow, which brought out the gold flecks in his eyes, and his gorgeous brown hair was combed straight back. "I really just want us to get along, Merry."

"How is that possible with you spreading things around behind my back?"

"I don't want anyone else getting in the way," Jon answered.

"Who're you talking about?" I said right out. "Is there someone you'd rather ask to the next youth outing? Is that it?"

He was shaking his head. "No, I hope *you'll* go with me, Merry."

I knew I had to set the record straight. He suspected Levi and I were getting too friendly. "You don't have to second-guess me, Jon. If you want to know why I've been spending so much time at Rachel Zook's, it's because of an orphan lamb."

His eyes softened. "A lamb?"

"That's right, and her name is Jingle Belle. She was desperate—dying—for a name, among other things. . . ."

By the time the homeroom bell rang, I'd told him the entire sad story. How Jingle needed me, how she wouldn't eat much for anyone else. How she was mourning her family.

"This is incredible," he said. "Why didn't you tell me last Monday?"

"I should've . . . I know."

He reached for my hand and held it. "Oh, Merry, forgive me?"

My heart nearly flipped out of my chest as he continued to hold my hand there in the hallway as the entire population of James Buchanan High filed by. "I'm sorry, too."

On my way to homeroom, I wondered how I could smooth things over with both Mom and Chelsea, too. I would definitely try. Still, I couldn't help but think Chelsea had meant to interfere. I was going to find out the truth. At lunch!

☙   ☙

I would give it my best shot with my outspoken girl friend. Chelsea was a new Christian, so I knew I must be very understanding toward her. I would close my mouth and open my ears—hear her out completely.

Searching the cafeteria, I saw her sitting alone. "Thank goodness, I found you," I said, nearly breathless as I scooted in next to her.

She kept chewing her sandwich, glancing at me out of the corner of her eyes.

"I don't know why you were so upset about the hike thing . . . and Jon and me," I began. "But it's okay now, he and I are cool. We talked."

She turned toward me. "It's just that I knew how crazy you were over him for such a long time. I couldn't stand by and let the two of you self-destruct." She went on to say that there were other girls in the youth group at church. "They've got their eyes on Jon."

"Plenty of girls do. I'm not stupid."

Chelsea nodded. "He's always been so 'out there'—on another planet somewhere—when it came to the opposite sex. I honestly thought he'd never figure out the girl-boy thing. But now with you and him together . . . well, it's almost too good to be true."

I agreed. "You don't have to worry. I haven't been avoiding Jon. He knows where I've been hanging out all week." Then I told *her* the lamb story.

She laughed out loud. "I don't believe this! You've been lamb-sitting?"

After further explanation, she seemed to understand. "I don't know about you, Mer. You've always been a little strange, but this. . . ?"

"Sometimes even I don't know about me," I muttered.

She didn't catch the tone of my remark, and I was glad. I really didn't care to explain my present mournful state. Knowing Chelsea, she might not understand that, either.

ELEVEN

After school, Jon showed up at my locker. He waited for me to collect my books, and then we walked to the bus. We sat together and talked all the way to SummerHill. When the bus stopped, I stood up to get off.

Jon jumped up. "Mind if I walk you home?"

I knew if he did, he'd have a long walk to his own house. "You don't have to," I said.

"But I *want* to, Merry." His smile softened my heart.

"Okay." Inside, I was secretly thrilled beyond words.

We took our sweet time walking up the hill that led to my parents' hundred-year-old farmhouse. Old, gnarled trees and the willow grove to the north surrounded us as we talked. "My sister used to think it would be fun to live in the woods," I told him.

"Faithie was really special," he replied. "I remember, in kindergarten, she painted a picture of a tree house."

I was shocked that he remembered. "You remember *that*?"

He nodded, his eyes smiling. "That, and lots more." He paused for a second. "Mostly I remember *you*, Mistress Merry."

"We've known each other nearly forever," I said, looking down at the road.

"I'm glad about that." He seemed shy just then.

"Me too," I said.

We talked of other school memories. Funny things that happened, and some not so funny. Later, Jon brought up the lamb at the Zooks'. "Sometime, I'd like to see her," he said.

"I thought you might want to take some pictures of Jingle. You know, for your photography class."

"That would be cool." He surprised me and reached for my hand. I have to admit I couldn't believe how fantastic it felt, holding hands with Jon again. At school and now here, on SummerHill Lane. I'd dreamed of this since forever, and now it was happening. I could hardly believe he'd decided to walk me home today. And I was pretty sure my mom would invite him in for her usual cookies and lemonade after-school menu.

"I'll ask Rachel if you can take some farm shots for your class next time I see her."

"That'd be great. Thanks."

"I don't think the Zooks will mind."

"Just so I don't focus on *them*, right?" Jon said.

I assured him it was a good idea to aim the lens only at the sheep. "You know how the Amish are about cameras. They despise having their pictures taken."

He laughed. "I've heard."

We slowed our pace as we approached the front yard of my house. At the mailbox, he stopped. "Merry, I think of you as my best friend." His eyes were shining. "I have for a long time."

"That's the nicest thing anyone's said to me." I felt completely comfortable admitting it.

"I think the Alliteration Game helped make the friendship connection stronger with you. You have no idea how shy I was back then—sorta had my head in the clouds, too. I'm glad we've moved on to a different level of friendship."

"Me too."

"You don't miss the Word Game, do you?" he asked, his eyes searching mine.

"Sometimes, but talking like this is much better."

I loved hearing his soft laughter. "You're the *best* friend I've ever had, Merry . . . or ever hoped to have."

I couldn't honestly say that back to him because of Faithie. She'd been my best friend, of course. "I've been hoping you'd say that ever since we sat across from each other in fourth grade."

He nodded. "Yeah, I remember. Guys don't really notice girls, I guess, till later on."

"Well, we found each other. That's what matters," I said, matching his stride as we headed up the front lawn and around the side to the back door. He gave my hand a gentle squeeze, then let go.

Mom was waiting on the back steps, smiling to beat the band. "Merry . . . Jon! Please come inside."

"You better be hungry," I whispered.

He chuckled and followed me into the kitchen.

I would've expected Mom to still be a little ticked at me. Instead, I was surprised by her enthusiasm. She seemed positively delighted to see me. And Jon, too.

The reason for her joy was forthcoming. Mom and Dad had spent their entire day discussing at length the ins and outs of running an antique dealership. And now my mother was sharing every conceivable tidbit of information with Jon and me. Whether we wanted to hear about it or not.

92

"It's going to be quite a venture," she said, offering the plate of cookies to Jon for the second time.

He was polite, of course, and listened to her babble on. Several times his gaze caught mine, and we shared a furtive glance. I was sure he was bored out of his mind, yet he sat there listening intently.

"Rachel Zook said she would help with your store if you ever need her," I said, making small talk.

"How sweet of her," Mom said. Then, quite unexpectedly, she added, "Speaking of Rachel, her brother dropped by this afternoon."

I gulped inwardly. *Not now, Mom!* I thought. *Don't talk about Levi in front of Jon!*

"Was Martha with him?" I asked, hoping she'd take the hint.

She looked puzzled, slowly catching on, I could only hope. "I didn't see her, no."

"Well, she's here visiting Levi's family," I managed to say. "Rachel thinks Levi and his girlfriend will soon be engaged."

Mom smiled at this news. "How lovely."

But it wasn't so lovely, her bringing up the subject of Levi Zook. Not today. Not after everything Jon and I had been through!

Still, the question remained: Why had Levi come here? Mom hadn't made that clear. But I remembered Rachel saying she was sure Levi would want to see me.

Sooner or later, I'd have to address the sticky situation with Jon. If I wanted to continue as his best friend, I'd have to. It just wasn't fair otherwise. Besides, I knew I wanted to see Levi again. For more than one reason.

TWELVE

"Mom, how *could* you?" I wailed the second Jon left. "I don't get it. You seemed relieved before that Levi was out of my life, then you bring him up . . . in front of Jon! It doesn't make any sense!"

She turned to the refrigerator and stood in the doorway for the longest time without speaking. "I'm sorry, Merry." She closed the refrigerator door and stood there, the gloomiest expression on her face. A stark contrast to the jovial face she'd worn minutes before while telling Jon and me about her day.

I wished I knew what to do. Stay and try to patch things up with Mom? Dad would probably say that was a good idea. But I was so angry with her. So terribly confused, too.

It would be easier for me to wander over to the Zooks' and busy myself there. Maybe check on

Jingle Belle. Or, who knows, maybe bump into Levi.

"What did Levi say when he came over?" I asked, more cautious now.

Mom ran some water and drank a sip out of a glass before answering. "It was quite obvious he was eager to see you, Merry. That's why he came."

"Why did you have to say anything in front of Jon?" I still saw no logical reason for it.

She shook her head. "You had just mentioned Rachel, and my mind leaped to Levi." She went to the table and sat down. "I don't know what's come over me lately." She began to whimper. "Sometimes I make the silliest mistakes—forget things, too. I'm worn out most of the time, but my doctor says it's typical."

Her doctor?

Suddenly, I felt truly horrible. I had no idea Mom was dealing with something physical. Dad had said it was a midlife crisis. Whatever that was. But by the sound of it, Mom was experiencing something worse. Why hadn't Dad told me?

"Oh, Mom, it's okay to cry," I said, going to her and stroking her hair. "I'm sorry . . . about everything. Honest. I shouldn't have talked to you that way at breakfast. I just didn't know."

She blubbered her response, and I had no idea what she said. But the air was definitely cleared between us. I had several more cookies and a glass of milk to wash them down. Before I left for the Zooks' farm, I kissed her. "I love you, Mom," I said.

"I love you, too, honey." Her tears were gone.

I felt much better, too.

❧   ❧

Rachel met me halfway between my house and hers. She said she'd been watching for me. Strands of hair at her neck were coming loose from her bun, and she was out of breath. "Merry, I was hopin' you'd come over." She seemed anxious.

"Everything all right?"

She shook her head. "Jingle's missing. Somehow, she got out of the fence."

I wondered if that was the reason for Levi's visit. But I didn't mention it. "Where'd you see her last?"

"She was near Ol' Nanna, like she might be gonna nurse from her . . . and then she just disappeared." Rachel hurried, her gait longer and faster than mine.

I scrambled to keep up with her. "Is there a place in the fence where she might've pushed through?"

"Honestly, I think she got out through the gate . . . maybe when Dat fed the older sheep."

"There aren't any wolves or other predators around, are there?" I asked.

She seemed more concerned about the lamb wandering too far away, forgetting how to get home. Maybe even starving to death. "Sheep are so dumb, ya know?"

I didn't know from experience, only from what I'd read in the Bible. "They're followers, right? They need a leader—a shepherd."

She nodded. "That's why we keep ours fenced in. At least, we *try* to."

The sun grew hotter as we ran together to the north meadow, out past the barn, beyond the pond. It was the same grassland where Rachel and I often gathered daisies and sat in the tall grass, sharing secrets. A wide expanse of land. Not the best place for a new lamb to roam freely. It was obvious why the entire Zook family had joined together to comb this section of land.

Just ahead, in the deepest grass, Levi and Martha were searching the meadow. To the right of them, Nancy, Ella Mae, and little Susie had joined hands, calling, "Jingle Belle, can you hear us?" over and over. Rachel's father and younger brother, Aaron, were looking, too. It would take hours to scour every inch of land. Most of the meadow remained untouched.

Rachel stopped to wipe her forehead. "How will we ever find Jingle?"

"We won't give up, that's how," I replied, forging ahead. I called out the name I'd chosen for the dear little lamb. "Jingle, where are you? Where *are* you?"

We kept at it, plodding through patches of meadow, even skirting the edge of the woods, looking, calling louder. I spotted a variety of wild and useful herbs and other plants along the way. And there were birds accompanying our journey. Sunshine played an important role in the search. I imagined Jingle's white wooly coat showing up clearly under the powerful spotlight of the sun's rays. If we could just find her before dark!

"Where would a baby lamb wander off to?" I said, stopping to catch my breath.

Rachel shook her head sadly. "That's just the thing . . . it's hard to know, really."

"She's got a mind of her own, that's for sure."

"Sheep are like that," she reminded me. Not giving up, Rachel kept moving through the grass. Her skirt hem brushed the tops of the foliage, and she kept her eyes on the ground.

I, on the other hand, glanced up ahead every so often. Occasionally, I caught sight of Levi and his girlfriend. They were working the field as a team. So were Rachel's younger sisters. Abe Zook and Aaron were way off in the outskirts of the meadow, still calling to the wayward lamb.

Suddenly, I thought of the Pied Piper. In a way, the lost lamb had been an invisible guide, leading us through the thickest grasses and trees. We were trying to follow an unseen trail. Then it occurred to me to look for a narrow path through the grass. "Wouldn't it be a good idea to look for smashed-down meadow grass?" I asked Rachel.

" 'Course it would. Gut thinking!"

So we turned around and did just that. We gazed back at the meadow from this side of the pond. I hoped to spot something to indicate that Jingle had wandered through the tallest grass.

"Do you see anything?" I asked.

"Nothin' at all." Rachel sounded discouraged.

"We'll find her," I assured her. "Count on me."

It was getting close to suppertime. My mother would be worried, especially if I didn't come home and she went to the Zooks' and found all of us gone. Except Esther, of course. Thank goodness, Rachel's mother had stayed behind. My mom would get the facts from her—where we were and why.

In the distance, I could see the north side of the Zooks' bank barn and pastureland. The willow grove was to the right of their property, creating a ridge—an obvious dividing line between their land and ours. It was an amazing sight; one I hadn't remembered seeing. "It's glorious," I said, scanning the horizon.

"Jah, the best part of livin' in the country. The wide, open spaces . . . and the woods."

I thought, just then, of the strange dream I'd had. Of being a maple tree, strong and true. No matter the wind or the weather, a tree like that stands tall. Was I *that* hardy? I truly wondered.

THIRTEEN

Low, slinky rain clouds hung in the sky on the far edge of SummerHill. Thunderbumpers, I'd nicknamed them. Soon, there would be distant thunder, but a change in weather was the farthest thing from my mind. A rain shower wouldn't spoil our search efforts, most likely. I, for one, wouldn't let a little moisture dampen my spirits. If need be, we could race the weather all the way home. We were going to find Jingle Belle if it took all night!

Another hour and a half passed quickly. Abe and Aaron and the younger girls headed back across the meadow toward the farmhouse. I wondered if Levi and Martha would do the same, but they persevered. So did Rachel and I. Dusk was coming on fast, and my stomach was growling out of control. It wouldn't be long till nightfall.

"We'd better head back. It's getting too dark now," Rachel said.

"You go ahead," I said. "I want to keep looking."

She peered up at the darkening sky. "Soon, you'll need a flashlight or a lantern."

"I have eyes like a cat. I can see in the dark." Then I remembered the moon. It had appeared just last night while I sat with my cats on the back step. "The moon's due out any minute."

"Not if those clouds keep comin'," she replied. There was apprehension in her voice.

"I'll be all right." I glanced up to see Levi and Martha still searching. "I'm in good company."

She smiled a weak smile and touched my arm. "You won't mind if I go, then?"

"I'm fine, honest."

She gave me a quick hug. "Maybe Jingle's wandered back to the corral already."

"Wouldn't someone ring the bell to let us know?"

"Jah, you're right." She turned to go, and I watched her for a few seconds before hurrying across the meadow. I decided to go in the opposite direction, away from Levi and Martha. It would be darker in the woods, but Jingle might've lost her way in there.

Time passed quickly. I lost track of how long it

had been since Rachel left, and I couldn't see my watch anymore. Dusk had come, and I could barely see where I was walking. Still, I was one-hundred-percent-amen sure I'd be able to see a flash of white wool, given the chance.

A long rumble of thunder rolled across the sky. There was no lightning, though, which would've helped me see. If only for an instant.

I thought of my cats, probably hiding under my bed or in my closet about now. Oh, they hated the sound of thunder! A fleeting, yet frightening thought crossed my mind. Who would comfort my cats if something happened to me—if I lost my way forever? If no one ever found *me*? I couldn't imagine Dad or Mom, either one, taking on the job of caring for my cat quartet. And my brother had always made fun of my need to take in strays. Skip didn't call me Cat Breath for nothing!

I could almost feel the dark clouds overhead, and I wished for a flash of lightning. Anything to guide me. "Jingle!" I called, again and again. "Can you hear me?"

There was not a sound but the crack of thunder. I forced myself to concentrate on finding the lost lamb. "I'm here for you, little girl," I said, clenching my fists. "I'm going to find you!"

The wind began to hit my face, and then came

the pelting rain. In no time, my face and hair were drenched. Thankfully, I was spared the full force of the pounding because of the dense trees. I knew better than to plant myself under one of them, though. The rainstorm was fierce, with flashes of light now cracking out of the sky like jagged white fingers. I was determined to find Jingle, yet I wanted to do the wise thing. I had to get far enough away from the trees. For safety from the lightning.

The thunder made my knees feel like rubber. Was I lost? I couldn't have wandered that far away. Could I?

In the underbrush, I heard a sound. The low bleating of an animal not far from me. "Jingle? Is that you?"

I followed the whimpering, determined to find her. A steady flicker of lightning aided me. There, in the thicket—caught in the brushwood—not more than three yards from me, was the little lamb.

"Oh, baby," I cried, crawling to her. "You'll be okay now. I'm here. Merry's here. . . ."

Her cries broke my heart, and I struggled to free her from the jungle of sharp vines. "Lord, help me," I whispered, snapping the briar that held her at last. In the process, I cut my fingers. But I couldn't determine how badly; I only felt the blood slowly oozing from my fingertips.

I sat on the wet ground, holding the lamb in my arms. Both of us were shaking hard. "Don't worry," I said, stroking her, holding her close. But my heart was beating ninety miles an hour.

After a time, Jingle began to relax. I continued to pet her and talk softly to her. The warmth of the lamb's body against my own comforted me. "The storm can't last forever," I said. "Storms never do."

That's when I remembered what Dad had said so often to me over the years. *"Only time will heal that kind of wound."*

"Time and . . . God's love, if we're patient," I said into Jingle's soft coat.

I remembered my strange but vivid dream— about me being a maple tree. My roots were deep, grounded in the soil of God's Word. Thanks to my parents' spiritual training and the teaching I'd received at church, nothing could knock me down. "Not even Faithie's death," I said aloud.

God had reminded me in a very unique way. Teamed up with Him, I was sturdy enough to face the future without my twin. I could trust God, just as this precious lamb in my lap could count on me to care for her through this truly horrible storm.

The storm won't last forever. . . .

My own words! And what truth they held for me. It was time to let go of the past. I had the ability, with

God's help, to move past the shadows. The truth hit me harder than the rain falling on my face.

"Thank you, Lord," I prayed, holding on to the lamb for dear life.

FOURTEEN

How long I sat there, I couldn't tell. After what seemed like hours, the rain finally slowed to a drizzle. It was still mighty dark, but I could see the shadow of the moon behind a cloud. I watched the sky, waiting breathlessly for the moon to become fully visible.

"We'll go home soon," I told Jingle. "We'll walk under the wonderful white moon."

For as long as it took—till we were rescued—I decided to play the Alliteration Word Game. Alone.

"God is here—hovering, holy, helpful," I began. "We'll be glad to get going—gleeful, giddy, and grateful to be home."

The wordplay was one way to keep my mind working. Pure genius! Far better than focusing on the frightening flashes far overhead, not to mention what foreign forest friends—or foes—might be furtively lurking.

Hugging the lamb in my arms, I continued. "Jingle Belle is beautiful, blessed, on her best behavior, both bright and brainy." I was running out of *b* words.

So I tried *f*, thinking jovial Jon would be jubilant just now. "Faithie was fantastic, fun-loving, fast, faithful, full of life . . ." I couldn't go on. Saying descriptive words about my twin made me cry. But my tears mingled with the rain on my face till it was impossible to tell which was which.

I thought of the summertime flowers that had refused to bloom after she died. And the horrible drought that followed. Most everything green had turned an ugly brown. When the rain finally did come that year, it seemed to come in buckets. Soon, life flowered around us again. Just as I believed my life without Faithie was going to blossom . . . from this night on.

It was getting late. A hoot owl startled me in a tree nearby, and I could hear rustling in the underbrush. Noises that were not the wind. I could only imagine what snakes and other crawling things might be out here.

Scared, I began to hum a song from church, wondering what songs they might play at my funeral if I should die here tonight. Purposely, I forced those thoughts out of my mind. I focused, instead, on God's sovereign will covering all His creation. That meant me, too! Merry Hanson trapped in a ferocious storm . . . lost in a deep and dark woods. Alone and afraid. Yet God's will covered me. I took true comfort in that.

Just then, a glimmer of light caught my eye. It was coming toward us, bobbing through the woods! Then I heard my name ringing through the trees. "Merry, can you hear me?"

It was Levi's voice! Courageous and strong.

"Over here!" I called back, still clinging to the lamb.

"Merry!"

Louder, I called back. "Levi . . . I'm here!"

Once the moon came out, he found me. His flashlight helped, too. "Oh, Merry," he said, bending down and shining the light in my face. "Are you all right?"

"My socks are soggy and most of me is soaking wet. But I found Jingle . . . and she's safe, too."

He reached down and helped me up, lamb and all. Faintly, I could see his face in the moonlight. "I was awful worried, Merry."

"I didn't think *you'd* come for me," I said, still totally amazed.

"Both your father and mine are searching. You gave us a fright, really you did."

"I'm okay, honest."

But he kept looking at me, as if he had to see for himself. "You've been crying. Merry . . ." Then, without waiting for me to answer, he brushed away my tears with the pads of his thumbs. "There," he whispered, "much better." Then, unexpectedly, he pulled me close, along with the lamb, into his arms. "I prayed you'd be all right," he was saying. "We all did."

"And I am," I assured him.

Levi released me gently, and we began to hike out of the woods, his flashlight guiding the way. His consoling hug had been a brotherly one. The old feelings, the romantic ones, had been replaced with something new.

He took the lamb from me, carrying her away from the woods toward the meadow. And as we walked, we talked of many things—my present school year . . . and his. How his brother, Curly John, and sister-in-law, Sarah, and their little Mary were doing. He also mentioned that his father had asked him to consider "joining church."

"But you're Mennonite," I insisted.

"Dat's stubborn as the day is long. Wants *all* his children in the Amish church."

"I'm sure you can understand why."

"But I've made a stand for the Lord by becoming a follower of Christ instead of the *Ordnung*." He was adamant about his newfound faith, and I was truly glad. Adjusting the lamb in his arms, he explained. "My father's from the Old Order—the old Amish way of doing things. He only knows what his father and grandfather before him passed on to him."

"And the bishop?"

"The bishop, too." He was quiet for a moment. "The fact is, unless someone witnesses to the Old Order folk, it's awful hard for them to hear the fullness of the Gospel. For one thing, the People aren't allowed to read the entire Bible. Only certain passages are encouraged, and those are preached over and over."

"How sad," I spoke up. "The Word of God holds all the answers for life's problems."

"And that's the truth!"

I remembered then that he'd dropped by to see me earlier. "Mom said you came over to the house."

"I couldn't leave SummerHill again without talking to you, Merry. Like the old days."

It was dear of him. "But those days are nearly gone," I gently reminded.

We kept our pace, moving through the tallest grassland now. "Martha said she met you," he said.

"Yes . . . and she's really terrific."

He laughed his joyful laugh—that warm and contagious chuckle I'd come to know so well. "Martha likes you, too."

"Maybe we'll become good friends," I said, hoping so.

"That might be difficult, since we're praying about going to South America as missionaries."

"When?"

"After graduation." He paused. "After I marry Martha."

The news didn't jolt me, not in the least. But it was mighty nice to hear it directly from Levi. "I know you'll be happy together," I said softly. "She's right for you, Levi."

The lamb jostled in his strong arms. "I hope you'll forgive me. I never wanted to hurt you."

I understood. "We were mistaken about the kind of love we had," I said. "I should've known you were more like a wonderful big brother. Nothing can change that."

"Still, I was wrong to lead you on. I said certain things . . . and I'm sorry."

"We're still friends, so don't worry."

"I'm glad you feel that way," he said, and I noticed he patted the lamb's head.

"Jingle's so adorable," I said. "She taught me

many things about myself . . . on the farm and back there in the woods. God allowed Jingle to come into my life for a reason. He allowed tonight's storm to happen, too. So I could learn to trust Him to quiet another, much bigger storm."

Levi listened patiently as I recounted my discoveries. He was kind, as always, and put up with my jabbering.

Once we were midway across the meadow, we started calling. Hollering, really. "Daddy, I'm alive!" I shouted.

We wanted my dad and Levi's, too, to know I'd been found.

"Merry's with me," Levi said, putting his free arm around my shoulder.

Merry's with me. . . .

A year ago, I might've replayed those words and this moment a thousand times in my mind. Tonight, I knew better. Levi was, and always would be, very special to me. But Martha was to be his life mate. I was truly happy for them.

❧   ❧

We stopped to let the lamb roam freely for a while, waiting for my dad and Abe Zook to catch up with us. "Miss Spindler's hooked up and turned on to the computer age," I told Levi. "Did Rachel tell you?"

He sat in the grass near the pond. "Well, she tried to, but honestly she lost me. Sounds like you finally did some snooping, though."

"I sure did. And it's the weirdest thing, especially for an elderly lady." I had to stop and laugh, recalling all the top-secret sleuthing that had gone on. "I even took a picture of her high-tech attic to prove it."

"Speaking of pictures, I have a request."

"Shoot."

"Well, I don't know how to ask this."

I had no idea what he was going to say.

"Would you be willing to take a picture of Martha and me for our engagement photo?"

I chuckled, not at the question, but at the idea of asking *me*. "A professional photographer might be a better choice, really. But thanks for the vote of confidence."

He shone his flashlight on Jingle, watching her play. "I've seen your work, Merry. You're very good."

"Well, if you're sure, then I'll be happy to take the picture."

"Would tomorrow work for you, near Mam's rose garden?"

"That'll be such a pretty backdrop. I'll come

over after school. Count on me," I said.

Our chatter turned to Miss Spindler again. "I notice you're not calling her your favorite nick-name," he said.

"Not anymore." I couldn't wait to tell him why. "Sure, she's a little peculiar. But I have to tell you, she was wonderful to me when I lost Abednego last month. I don't know how I would've found my cat without her help."

"Sounds like things are changing mighty fast around SummerHill," he said, getting up and chasing Jingle playfully.

Well, I had news for him. Miss Spindler wasn't the only one. "My mom wants to start an antique shop," I told him. "Can you believe it?"

"Rachel said something about that. Sounds interesting."

"I'm trying to get used to the idea. It's a little strange, I have to admit."

"How's your friend Jon Klein?" he asked out of the blue.

I wondered how to describe Jon to Levi without sounding like a girl in love. "Well, let's see . . ."

Levi carried the lamb over and sat down beside me again. "I'm all ears."

"Jon's not the Alliteration Wizard anymore, so that's another change. But he's taking a photography class, which means we have cameras and lenses and pictures in common."

"You're skirting the issue," said Levi, laughing. "I asked a simple question."

"And you want a simple answer, right?"

I looked up at the sky, wondering if tonight was the right time. "This is just between you and me, okay?"

"I promise."

I took a deep breath. These were precious words. "I think Jon and I are becoming best friends."

"That's just what I hoped you'd say, Merry."

I was one-hundred-percent-amen happy!

❧   ❧

Dad and I walked home the rest of the way together. I thought of the events of the evening. How I'd lost my way, trying to find a missing lamb. I thought, too, of the changes occurring between Levi and me. Between Levi and his own dear family.

Some of the biggest changes had taken place inside me. And I knew I was ready to talk to Mom about Faithie. I could hardly wait!

FIFTEEN

Mom was terribly worried about the cuts on my fingers. She hovered near me as I ran cold water over them at the kitchen sink. Then she insisted on using hydrogen peroxide to cleanse away any possible infection. On top of that, she made me get out of my drenched clothes and put on warm, dry ones. All this before we ever sat down to supper.

My cats seemed happier than usual to see me, too. "Guess I should get caught in a rainstorm more often," I teased.

Mom gave me a sideways look, which meant my comment was ridiculous. "Let's pray and eat," she said.

With bandaged fingers, I took my place at the table. Leave it to Mom to keep the meal hot after all this time. I could tell Dad was mighty glad. He stopped to relish almost every bite. Mom got a big kick out of it. But more than that, she seemed eager to dote on me, obviously thrilled that I was safe. "I'm so glad you're home, Merry," she went on and on.

"What a night to remember," I said, grinning at both Dad and Mom.

Mom shook her head. "Well, I can't imagine being lost out in that vicious storm . . . and wandering around in the woods!"

"God answered our prayers for Merry," Dad said, interjecting a positive remark.

"We're so glad He did!" Mom offered me more mashed potatoes and gravy. Instead of refusing, I actually took a second helping, recalling how cold and lonely—and terribly frightened—I'd felt just a few hours before.

It was truly good to be home.

❧   ❧

While Mom and I cleaned up the kitchen, I brought up the subject of her clothesline. "I wondered if you'd thought about it . . . with customers coming, and all."

"I don't mind if *they* don't," she said. Then, smiling at me, she added, "Even if they object, it's staying!" She tossed a dish towel at me, and I began to dry the pots and pans. I wanted to make it easy for Mom to talk about Faithie, but hesitated, hoping for the right time.

"Your friend Ashley Horton called during the storm," Mom said.

"I don't believe this! Every time I'm gone, someone calls."

"You have a busy life . . . and that's a good thing."

"What's on Ashley's mind?" I asked.

"She's having a sleepover this weekend. She said Chelsea and Lissa were planning to go."

"What'd you tell her?"

She stopped to look at me, her deep brown eyes now very serious. "I told her that you were your own social planner. That you'd return her call."

"Thanks, Mom. You're so cool."

Her eyes widened. "So . . . I'm evolving? To *cool*?"

"Yep."

"Well, hearing that makes my day," she said, turning back to the sudsy sink.

I finished drying one of the pans. Then, all at once, tears began to cloud my vision. I sniffled a little, trying to keep them under control. "Mom, you made *my* day," I said, "the day you gave birth to Faithie and me. . . ."

"Oh, honey." She dropped her dishcloth and wrapped me in her arms.

"I thought I was the one . . . who hurt the most . . . when my sister died," I said, sobbing. "But Faithie and I grew inside you. You gave us life. *You* lost your baby girl!"

Both of us were crying now. Thank goodness Dad didn't stroll through the kitchen just then. Except, if he had, he would've discovered a mother and daughter sharing their deepest pain. Their loss. And best of all, their most precious memories.

Honestly, it was easy to do the thing Dad had requested of me. I openly talked to Mom about Faithie. Even grabbed her hand and took her upstairs. I closed the door in my room and sat her down on my bed, propping her up with pillows. At first, she wasn't too thrilled about having the cats join us for a tender look back into the past. Our past.

But it didn't take long before she was oblivious to the cats curled up around her. What a long time since I'd invited Mom or anyone to see my scrapbooks. So I took things slow and easy, sharing each memory—even the tiniest one—as it came to me.

Mom, too, had meaningful things to say about each picture. Some things I'd completely forgotten or, better yet, never known. "Faithie insisted on parting her hair on the opposite side to yours," Mom said, pointing to a picture to demonstrate the point.

I nodded, staring at it. "Sometimes I actually got the feeling Faithie resented being a twin."

Mom's arm was around me again. "Your sister was a very independent little girl. But she adored you. And you must surely know that is true."

"Sometimes I wish I had more gumption," I confessed. "Like Faithie did."

Mom turned to the next page. "God made the two of you completely unique. No one knows that better than your father and I. And we loved you both dearly." She went on to recite various incidents when Faithie had exerted her strong will.

I slid around the side of the bed so I could look at Mom as she talked. In the end, I spent more time gazing at her face than at the scrapbook. After all, I'd nearly memorized the pages. But it had been a long time since I'd truly concentrated on my mother.

"This storm is coming to an end, isn't it?" I recalled the words I'd said to comfort the lamb in the forest.

Mom was very still. Then she got up and walked across the room to my bookcase. She reached for my Bible and opened to Psalm 71. "Listen to this, honey," she said, reading to me. " 'For you have been my hope, O Sovereign Lord, my confidence since my youth. From birth I have relied on you; you brought me forth from my mother's womb. I will ever praise you . . . you are my strong refuge.' "

I let the words sink in. How amazing they were!

Our eyes met and locked. "God is our refuge in the storms of life," she said. "He protected us, as He always will." She sighed, closing the Bible. "Yes, Merry, I believe the storm is past."

SIXTEEN

Jingle Belle took her milk from Ol' Nanna on Friday afternoon. She had graduated from the nursing bottle to a new "mama." A triumph!

I asked Rachel if Jon Klein could come for a visit "to take some pictures around the farm."

She agreed. "That's fine. Anyone who's a friend of yours is welcome here."

I was almost sure she'd feel that way. "Jon's eager to see Jingle," I told her, following her around the side of the brick farmhouse.

"Sounds like her fame is spreading," she replied, straightening her long apron. "I'd say we've got ourselves a perty gut little lamb, don'tcha think?"

"She's healthy . . . she survived the storm. And now, looks like Ol' Nanna's just what the doctor ordered."

"Jah, Dr. Merry." Giggling about it, Rachel took me around the side of the house. We strolled past colorful flower beds of petunias, marigolds, and pansies of every imaginable hue. But it was in Esther Zook's rose garden that Levi and Martha were waiting to have their picture taken.

I made sure the sun was at my back, even though it shone in their eyes a bit. From experience, I knew that kind of lighting would produce the best results. "I never take just one shot," I explained.

Rachel said, "She's right," but didn't say how she knew. Truth was, I'd taken numerous pictures of her last winter before she decided to settle down and follow the Amish ways. Levi, of course, had other plans—which didn't include the Old Order rules and regulations. So he posed nicely with his bride-to-be, and I snapped away. Not once did I feel a twinge of sadness for losing my friend Levi to Martha Martin. As the Plain folk liked to say, their love for each other was ever so *providential*.

❧   ❧

I found Mom and Miss Spindler cleaning out the potting shed when I returned. They'd already swept out the dirt and cobwebs—shined up the little windows, too. Dad was nailing up window boxes all around, and I spied the red geranium plants just itching to be planted. The place was going to be as quaint and cute as any antique shop in all of Lancaster County.

"Merry, dearie," Miss Spindler called. "Come have a look-see at this here curtain fabric."

I stepped inside the shed-turned-store. She was holding up a soft, yellow-striped fabric in one hand, a busy floral in the other. Her blue-gray hair was perfectly coifed in her usual puffed-up do. Her face shone with a radiant joy, the same sort of delight she'd displayed last month when Rachel presented her with a gray kitten.

I eyed the fabric. It was an easy choice. "Definitely the stripes," I said, imagining the room painted and furnished with display tables.

"Merry's partial to stripes," Mom told Miss Spindler.

Miss Spindler tilted her head. "Oh, is that so?"

I nodded. "You should see my room. Stripes are everywhere."

"Well, to tell you the honest truth, I think the floral material is a little too much." Ruby Spindler grinned broadly.

Mom was smiling, too. "Thanks for your input, Merry."

"Anything else I can help with?" I offered, noticing Miss Spindler's kitten had wandered into the yard and was about to encounter Abednego—king of kitties! "Yee-ikes," I said, buzzing off to avert a *cat*astrophe!

Quickly, I scooped up the kitten. My big cat arched his black furry back and hissed. "That's not polite," I scolded him. "You've got company today."

Meow! Abednego protested, still arched and ready for a hissy fit.

"You need to mind your manners, young man," I continued. "We're going to have many more visitors pretty soon. *Customers*."

My oldest cat wasn't too wild about that information. He turned and slinked low like he was checking around for a mouse-y meal. Then he made a beeline for the gazebo. His most favorite hide-out.

"Sorry about that, little one," I whispered to the kitty. "Abednego thinks he simply *has* to be top dog at all times."

"Who're you talking to?" Mom said, poking her head out of one of the windows in her new shop.

I held up the kitten. "Miss Spindler's kitty-cat. What's her name, anyway?" I asked.

Mom disappeared momentarily. Soon, both Mom and Miss Spindler were smiling at me. "She doesn't have a name yet," our neighbor said. "What's she look like to *you*, dearie? Is she a Gertie or a Missy?"

"Neither one," I said, taking a good look at her. "Shadow. She looks like a shadow."

Mom clapped her hands. "You're right!"

Miss Spindler agreed. "Then *Shadow* it is."

I sat in the grass, soaking up the sunshine with little Shadow in my lap. "Life is full of sunshine and shadows," I said. "You're a good reminder for all of us."

The kitten looked up at me and smiled. Well, at least, I *think* it was a smile.

❧   ❧

Ashley Horton, our pastor's daughter, gave me the biggest hug ever when I arrived at her house for the sleepover. "We're going to play the Word Game tonight," she announced.

Chelsea was nodding, her arms folded across her chest. "She's not kidding, Mer. Ashley's not going to let us sleep till we each come up with at least four words in a row."

"They have to make a sentence," Lissa said, her hair in a perky ponytail.

I put down my overnight case. "Well, let's see . . ."

"Wait a minute. There's one minor detail missing from this assignment," Ashley said, twirling her hair with her finger. "The alliteration has to be about a boy."

"Oh, not *that*!" Chelsea pretended to choke herself.

I let the others play the game for a while, thinking back to all the energy I'd put into the word wars with Jon for almost two years. The girls might not understand why I'd abandoned the bantering. But it had nothing to do with them.

As I listened to Lissa trying to alliterate four words, I couldn't wait to invite Jon to see Jingle. To take pictures of the darling lamb and Ol' Nanna. Maybe I'd take my camera, too, and secretly shoot Jon taking a picture! What a weird and wacky photo that would be!

I must've been smiling because Ashley threw a pillow at me. "You're daydreaming, Merry. So . . . it's your turn!"

I thought for a moment. Could I do it?

"Remember, it has to be about a boy," Ashley reminded me, sitting cross-legged on the floor.

"Levi loves life lots," I said.

Lissa burst out laughing, but Ashley was silent. "How does she do that?" Ashley said.

Chelsea looked solemn. "Levi's leaving?"

"Mennonite Martha Martin may be marrying my man. . . ."

130

"*Your* man?" Lissa gasped. "Surely you don't mean—"

"No, I'm not brokenhearted. Not at all," I explained, abandoning the game. "I'm actually happy for Levi and Martha."

"So . . . are you saying you met her?" Chelsea asked.

"I took their engagement pictures in the Zooks' rose garden this afternoon," I said.

"No way," Chelsea replied.

"The proof's right here." I dug into my purse and waved the film canister.

They were all bug-eyed. Like they couldn't believe it.

"Make some alliteration about Jon Klein," Ashley said, eyes wide.

I shook my head. "I could, but I won't. How I feel about Jon is private stuff."

Lissa and Chelsea were grinning at me. "*Oooh*, I guess we know where Merry stands with the Kleinman," Chelsea teased.

They burst into laughter, but I didn't mind. Tomorrow I would invite Jon to meet Jingle Belle. And if it was an exceptionally beautiful day, I would take my tripod along and make a picture of the three of us.

I could just see it now. . . .

SEVENTEEN

It was amazing! Both Ashley and Chelsea were able to get up to four words in a row by midnight. Lissa didn't mind that she made it to only *three* words. When all was said and done, we talked and giggled and ate popcorn till we were so tired we couldn't keep our eyes open anymore.

As for Jon, I had the best time showing him around the Zooks' dairy farm the next day. We explored every nook and cranny in the barn. And my favorite place in the world: the hayloft. He took oodles of pictures—mules, hand-hewn plows, even the barn rafters. I had to laugh, wondering if maybe Jon was becoming a little *too* interested in farm life.

He and I spent an hour playing with Jingle Belle. (Jon really likes my name for the lamb!) He also helped me set up the tripod for a picture. It turned out so good, Mom suggested I frame it. So I'm going to hang it in my photo gallery, on my bedroom wall. That way, I'll never forget the special day.

I have a feeling there are lots more days like that ahead. Jon and I are becoming best friends. A true and caring friendship is a "good, solid basis for a possible dating relationship," Dad said the other night.

"When the time comes," Mom added. Of course.

I'm going along with Jon and his photography club to the Susquehanna River, after all. He asked if I'd bring *my* camera, too. "You could be president of the club, Merry. You're a natural," he said, flashing his winning smile.

Just between the two of us, our interests have switched to photography in a really big way. Maybe someday we'll return to the Word Game, but for now photography's the thing!

Dad says I'm old enough to start making decisions about who I spend time with. It's great to know he trusts me. And I won't disappoint him or Mom, that's for sure.

The Antique Shoppe is darling, and we've already had more than twenty customers in just three days. Not a single one has mentioned the clothesline. In fact, my mother puts it to good use, displaying old doilies and quilted table runners. Pure genius!

Nearly every evening, I spend time with Mom. She and I have gotten much closer this summer. We've been baking zucchini bread and selling it. When I told Rachel about some of the baked goods we were marketing, she raised her eyebrows. I guess we *are* giving our Amish neighbors some competition.

Skip's home from college for the summer. It's actually great having my brother underfoot again. He still calls me disgusting names that allude to my cat obsession, but overall he's becoming a cool guy. Guess that's what growing up does for an obnoxious older brother.

Last I heard, Levi formally proposed to Martha Martin. The *Lancaster New Era* ran their engagement announcement, complete with the photo I took of them. I'm a bona fide published photographer at last!

One of the Zooks' cats had another litter. Rachel brought over a darling yellow kitten as a thank-you for nursing Jingle back to health. I knew better than to ask Mom. Still, the kitten reminds me of a drop of sunshine. I'm thinking of talking to Miss Spindler about taking another pet. It would be so cute: Sunshine and Shadow, purring together under the same roof.

Sunshine and Shadow . . . That's also the name of a very popular Pennsylvania Amish quilt pattern. It says a lot about life.

I've accepted my share of shadows. Without them, I probably wouldn't appreciate the sunshine. With God's help, I've come a long way since I set up the before-and-after pictures in a SummerHill cemetery.

A truly long way.

FROM BEVERLY ... TO YOU

❧   ❧

I'm delighted that you're reading SUMMERHILL SECRETS. Merry Hanson is such a fascinating character—I can't begin to count the times I laughed while writing her humorous scenes. And I must admit, I always cry with her.

Not so long ago, I was Merry's age, growing up in Lancaster County, the home of the Pennsylvania Dutch—my birthplace. My grandma Buchwalter was Mennonite, as were many of my mother's aunts, uncles, and cousins. Some of my school friends were also Mennonite, so my interest and appreciation for the "plain" folk began early.

It is they, the Mennonite and Amish people—farmers, carpenters, blacksmiths, shopkeepers, quiltmakers, teachers, schoolchildren, and bed and breakfast owners—who best assisted me with the research for this series. Even though I have kept their identity private, I am thankful for these wonderfully honest and helpful friends.

If you want to learn more about Rachel Zook and her people, ask for my Amish bibliography when you write. I'll send you the book list along with my latest newsletter. Please include a *self-addressed, stamped envelope* for all correspondence. Thanks!

Beverly Lewis
℅ Bethany House Publishers
11400 Hampshire Ave. S.
Minneapolis, MN 55438

Also by Beverly Lewis

PICTURE BOOK

Cows in the House

THE CUL-DE-SAC KIDS
Children's Fiction

The Double Dabble Surprise	*The Crabby Cat Caper*
The Chicken Pox Panic	*Tarantula Toes*
The Crazy Christmas Angel Mystery	*Green Gravy*
No Grown-ups Allowed	*Backyard Bandit Mystery*
Frog Power	*Tree House Trouble*
The Mystery of Case D. Luc	*The Creepy Sleep-Over*
The Stinky Sneakers Mystery	*The Great TV Turn-Off*
Pickle Pizza	*Piggy Party*
Mailbox Mania	*The Granny Game*
The Mudhole Mystery	*Mystery Mutt*
Fiddlesticks	*Big Bad Beans*

GIRLS ONLY (GO!)
Youth Fiction

Dreams on Ice	*A Perfect Match*
Only the Best	*Reach for the Stars*
Follow the Dream	

HOLLY'S HEART SERIES
Youth Fiction

Holly's First Love	*Straight-A Teacher*
Secret Summer Dreams	*The "No-Guys" Pact*
Sealed With a Kiss	*Little White Lies*
The Trouble With Weddings	*Freshmen Frenzy*
California Christmas	*Mystery Letters*
Second-Best Friend	*Eight Is Enough*
Good-bye, Dressel Hills	*It's a Girl Thing*

Adult Fiction

The Postcard	*The Crossroad*
The Sunroom	

THE HERITAGE OF LANCASTER COUNTY

The Shunning *The Confession*

The Reckoning

Girls Like You—
PURSUING
OLYMPIC
DREAMS!

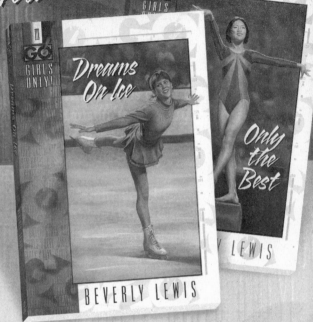

Don't miss the new series of books from Beverly Lewis called GIRLS ONLY (GO!). In this fun-loving series, you'll meet Olympic hopefuls like Livvy, Jenna, and Heather, girls training to compete in popular Olympic sports like figure-skating, gymnastics, and ice-dancing. Along the way, they tackle the same kinds of problems and tough choices you do—with friends and family, at school and at home. You'll love cheering on these likable girls as they face life's challenges and triumphs!

POPULAR WITH SPORTS-MINDED GIRLS EVERYWHERE!

GIRLS ONLY (GO!)
Dreams on Ice
Only the Best
Perfect Match

Available from your nearest Christian bookstore
(800) 991-7747 or from Bethany House Publishers.

Early Teen Fiction Series From Bethany House Publishers

(Ages 11–14)

———— ∞∞∞ ————

BETWEEN TWO FLAGS • by Lee Roddy
Join Gideon, Emily, and Nat as they face the struggles of growing up during the Civil War.

THE ALLISON CHRONICLES • by Melody Carlson
Follow along as Allison O'Brian, the daughter of a famous 1940s movie star, searches for the truth about her past and the love of a family.

HIGH HURDLES • by Lauraine Snelling
Show jumper DJ Randall strives to defy the odds and achieve her dream of winning Olympic Gold.

SUMMERHILL SECRETS • by Beverly Lewis
Fun-loving Merry Hanson encounters mystery and excitement in Pennsylvania's Amish country.

THE TIME NAVIGATORS • by Gilbert Morris
Travel back in time with Danny and Dixie as they explore unforgettable moments in history.